WHAT WOULD YOU DO WITH A SCROOGE?

Professional holiday decorator Natalie Fiorre loves tinsel, gingerbread, and the magic of Christmas. She believes there isn't anything in the world that a dash of Christmas Spirit can't fix—until she meets Gabe.

Perpetual Scrooge Gabe Cavanaugh loathes candy canes, jingle bells, and all things merry and bright. He believes Christmas is the *worst* time of year.

So when Miss Christmas and Mr. Scrooge meet, sparks fly.

When Gabe threatens to evict Natalie and her neighbors on Christmas she does what any right-minded Christmas-lover would do...

Natalie has two days to stop the evictions and help Gabe

discover the magic of Christmas, but a lot can go wrong in two days, and in Romeo, the soul mate capital, there's another kind of magic in the air.

A delightfully cheeky rom com romp through the holidays, Scrooging Christmas is Book Seven in the Soul Mates in Romeo Romance Series by Sarah Ready.

ALSO BY SARAH READY

Stand Alone Romances:

The Fall in Love Checklist

Hero Ever After

Once Upon an Island

Josh and Gemma Make a Baby

Josh and Gemma the Second Time Around

Soul Mates in Romeo Romance Series:

Chasing Romeo

Love Not at First Sight

Romance by the Book

Love, Artifacts, and You

Married by Sunday

My Better Life

Scrooging Christmas

Stand Alone Novella:

Love Letters

Find these books and more by Sarah Ready at:

www.sarahready.com/romance-books

scrooging christmas

SARAH READY

W.W. CROWN BOOKS
An imprint of Swift & Lewis Publishing LLC
www.wwcrown.com

Published by W.W. Crown Books an Imprint of Swift & Lewis Publishing, LLC, Lowell, MI USA
Cover Illustration & Design: Elizabeth Turner Stokes
Interior Illustration: Adobe Stock 293037949
Chapter Heading Images: Adobe Stock 303326174

Library of Congress Control Number: 2022915669
ISBN: 978-1-954007-67-3 (eBook)
ISBN: 978-1-954007-57-4 (pbk)
ISBN: 978-1-954007-58-1 (large print)
ISBN: 978-1-954007-59-8 (hbk)

scrooging christmas

PROLOGUE
GABE

December 21, 11:12 p.m.

The Christmas carols are horridly, ear-numbingly loud. The sleigh bells, the trilling trumpet, and the joyful voices boomerang inside my skull and jolt me out of unconsciousness.

I lie still, my cheek scratching against cheap, prickly carpet, the scent of pine and gasoline sharp in my nose as I struggle to brush aside the veil of confusion.

Darkness coats my vision, thick, and absolute. There's the taste of fresh falling snow in the air, mixed with the copper tang of blood on my dry lips.

So, there's snowfall.

Pine trees.

The icy darkness of the cramped trunk.

My knees are tucked against my chest. Hot needles

prick at my calves just above my tied ankles. My wrists are bound behind my back.

I wriggle my numb fingers, rotate my hands. It's not rope, handcuffs, or zip ties that hold me, it's...Christmas lights?

I'm tied up with the green cordage of a hundred Christmas bulbs?

The plastic cord digs into my wrists and ankles, cutting off circulation as I struggle. The trunk is coffin-like, too tight to maneuver.

You'd think, if you were bent on stuffing a six-foot-two man inside a trunk, you'd find a car bigger than a roller skate. But I'm trussed up like a Christmas goose, stuck in an oven. Except this oven is a trunk and achingly cold. The sharp icicle teeth of December bite at my nose and cheeks.

The crunch of ice-filled potholes and snow grinding under the car tires is muted beneath the chirpy high-pitched chorus of Christmas cheer. The carols assault my ears, but I listen for the sounds beyond the singing.

The night is curiously quiet, there's only the music, the grumble of the engine, the tires crunching over ice-coated snow, and the claustrophobic noise of my own breathing.

I'm not in Manhattan then. Not anywhere near my apartment.

The car jostles around a curve and I roll and slide into the trunk wall, crushing my face against the unyielding metal surface.

A package bumps into my back, brushing against my

hands. Wrapping paper, a frilly bow, I run my fingers over the slick paper surface.

I'm in the trunk with a present.

My stomach rolls as we round another curve, bumping over a small hill. I'm on a country road, far, far from home, that much is clear.

I jerk about and try to dislodge my cell from my suit pocket. Thirty seconds in I realize my phone isn't in my pocket. I can't feel the thick bulge of my wallet either.

I draw in a deep breath of stagnant air and tell myself to think...think...think.

They have to be after money. A million? Two? More?

I grit my teeth, the bitter smell of Christmas pine and snow lingering in my nose.

I don't remember anything after hailing the taxi. Is that it then? Did the taxi driver render me unconscious and shove me into their trunk?

I try to recall their appearance, to picture who is currently at the wheel, driving us farther and farther away from New York. But I can't. When I rifle through my memories, looking for their face, I only see a blank empty space.

I kick at the area where the tail light is. Maybe if I knock it out I can signal another car. But the only thing that comes of my efforts is an aching ankle.

I hate Christmas.

I really, really hate Christmas.

And wouldn't it be just the figgy pudding to top it all if I died out in the snowy, pine tree wilds, in the car of some Christmas carol loving maniac?

A curious calm settles over me, the pine needle smell tickling my nose, my heartbeat slowing to the lull of "Silent Night."

The car slows, crawling along at five miles an hour, winding down, I assume, a long country drive, deep in some craggy, forgotten woods.

This is it then.

My skin prickles from the icy cold, my blood pumps loud like a drum in my ears, the tang of gasoline and blood coats my mouth.

The car stops.

"Silent Night" cuts out mid note.

I hold still, barely allowing myself to breathe, listening. My muscles tense and a surge of adrenaline crashes through me.

The night is silent. It's the silence that comes after a deep, wistful snowfall blankets the earth. For now, everyone and everything is quiet.

Then the front car door opens with a loud, pained creak, its hinges rusted and misused.

I lift my head, the carpet roughing my cheek as I turn toward the noise of snow crunching under boots. The car door slams like a gunshot and I stiffen.

This is it.

When they open the trunk, I'll catapult at them, knock them aside, wrestle them to the ground, try...well, I'll do whatever I can to overpower them.

I'm not easy prey. I'm not going down without a fight. No matter that I'm tied hand and foot. I won't make this easy for them. No matter what, I'll fight. I promise that.

Another footstep through the snow. I grip my right hand into a fist and strain at the ties. Another footstep.

Who are they? What do they want?

Another footstep, closer, the snow loud beneath their boots.

Why did it have to be Christmas?

I bite my tongue and shove down the unwelcome vision of a crooked Christmas tree decorated with a red and green paper chain, the scent of popcorn strung on thread, gingerbread baking in the oven, and the sound of laughter and "Deck the Halls" banged out on an out of tune piano.

They take three shuffling steps closer and pause at the trunk. And I realize the gingerbread smell isn't a ghost from my memory, it's them.

I can smell them through the trunk, the gingerbread flavor lingers mockingly on my tongue.

A cold chill grips me and I prepare to lunge. Escape.

They stand there for five seconds.

Ten.

Twenty.

I can hear them breathing—loud, nervous pants.

Thirty.

They scuff their boots in the snow.

Suddenly, the trunk lid flies open.

The swirling cold wind bites me.

I don't wait to orient myself. I jerk upright, lunge forward.

But instead of making a heroic leap, I hit the edge of the trunk and hurtle into the hard snow and ice drive.

The air knocks from my lungs and I gasp, struggling to draw in the freezing, dry air.

The night is deep, deep dark. Lit only by stars and a sliver of cold moonlight.

The silent air presses at me, as if it's that terrifying eternal moment, between the exhale and the inhale.

Finally, I drag in a shuddering breath. My lungs fill with the flavor of bitter cold snow, cedar and pine, and yes, gingerbread, coated in sugary icing.

I struggle upright, digging my hands into the icy, hard-packed snow, and kick my tied ankles so that I move away from my abductor.

The snow bites my hands and the slick ice hisses as I scramble back. I fall over a snow bank and land in a ditch.

The soft snow exhales as I sink into the freshly fallen fluff, half-buried with a quiet whoosh. The snow has a peculiar way of dampening every noise.

I growl and bare my teeth as I turn to confront whoever was foolish enough to take me from Manhattan, shove me in a trunk, and bring me here. Wherever I am.

This is it.

Then, in the silver moonlight—tiny needle points of falling snow sparkling like crystals in the dark—I see her.

It's lucky I'm already on the ground because seeing her hits me like the winds of a Nor'easter, ripping roofs off in a gale of destruction.

She's backlit by the moon and lit by the obnoxiously

flashing red and green Christmas bulb earrings and necklace she's wearing.

There's a reason she smells like gingerbread and Christmas spice. She's Miss Christmas personified.

I curl my lip and blast her with an icy, contemptuous stare.

She's in a red velvet dress that strokes her curves, a handmade snowflake scarf, and black winter boots topped with soft white fur.

There's a halo of snow around her head, and she looks like a Christmas angel, or devil, more like.

Her bright red lips probably taste like candy canes stirred in hot chocolate, but I swear I'll never know whether they do or not. Because this woman is trouble. She's worse than trouble.

Her lips turn up, she smiles at me and waves, like she's Mrs. Claus at the Thanksgiving Day parade.

Her dark, wildly curly hair, her freckles, her button nose, they all shout innocence. But there's nothing innocent about her.

"You," I growl, lacing that one word with everything I hate about Christmas, about Christmas spirit, and about this woman who thinks she can tie me up and cart me off to who knows where. "You are going to rot in prison for a very, very, very long time."

She laughs. It's low, throaty, and warm like a mulled cider in front of a toasty fire.

Her laugh strokes me and hits me down low, where even sitting in a freezing snow bank and loathing her with everything I am, I can't stop my body from reacting.

Her smile spreads into a wide kid-on-Christmas-morning kind of grin and her eyes light up like the Christmas bulb earrings flashing at her ears.

Her nose crinkles with her smile and she walks over to the snow bank, her boots scraping over the snow. She puts her hands on her hips, and leans over me. Her warm breath puffs out in a whispery cloud curling between us.

Her candy cane-red lips purse together and then she winks. "Ho, ho, ho, Scrooge. And a Merry Christmas to you too."

1

NATALIE

ON CHRISTMAS EVE WHEN I WAS TEN, MY DAD TOLD ME, "Natalie, there isn't anything in the whole world that can't be cured by a bit of Christmas spirit."

That promise held absolutely, undoubtedly, one hundred percent true—until today.

The office of Cavanaugh and Sons is Christmas heaven.

Only a few hours ago the depressing space in Midtown was all beige and gray and boring.

As soon as you walked through the front door you were confronted by endless rows of cramped cubicles, the chemical scent of printer toner, and staff with their heads down clicking on keyboards.

There wasn't any talking or smiling—you could feel your soul being siphoned away under the ugly fluorescent lights. The whirring sound of a paper shredder filled the air, and I could only think, *that is the sound of dreams being shredded.*

So I fixed it.

I sprinkled Christmas spirit everywhere.

Ta da!

Now the cubicles are lined with yards and yards of glittering balsam fir garland and red velvet bows. There are hundreds of Christmas bulbs casting a warm glow over the office space, inviting happy conversation and joy.

I hung mistletoe, bright green holly, and Christmas bulb wreaths and set out crystal dishes full of candy canes and Christmas chocolates.

The fresh, lovely scent of balsam and pine mixes with the warm cinnamon and ginger smell of my homemade, candy-coated, sugar icing gingerbread house. The gumdrops, peppermint drops and licorice ropes are so sweet and the gingerbread so fragrant you can taste it in the air.

As the final bit of happiness, there's a fifteen-foot-tall Christmas tree, glittering with silver garland, silver Christmas bulbs, white twinkling lights, and a shining silver star on top.

The tree is positioned near the employee break room —where I placed trays of Christmas cookies, a five-gallon thermos of rich hot cocoa, and a stereo piping out the delightful jingling of sleigh bells.

The offices of Cavanaugh and Sons is my pièce de résistance. I have never ever decorated an office space with such magical splendor. I've also never seen such a transformation.

The formerly dour, silent employees are now chatting, smiling, perhaps...dreaming. There's music, laughter, warmth.

It's happy.

Or...it was.

The man stalks down the long rows of cubicles, head and shoulders above everyone else.

He's in a form-fitting black suit, crisp and severely cut. His eyes are dark and cold, like a winter night full of ice and snow.

His hair is black like the deepest midnight, starless and sleek. His jaw is hard, his lips unsmiling, and the way he stares straight ahead, at me—only me—makes me freeze, like he's pressed pause and I can't move until he pushes play again.

My pulse flutters in my neck, and by the way he narrows his eyes, I swear he can see my reaction.

As he stalks down the aisle, people drop suddenly into their chairs, stop speaking mid-conversation, or scurry to hide their cookies (by tossing them in the trash or shoving them in their mouths).

As soon as he strides within shouting distance, people jerk back with shock and then wipe away all that Christmas cheer. It's like he's a villain with a freeze ray. Or an anti-Christmas-joy ray.

The reaction would be comical if it weren't so clear that he's the boss.

Finally he reaches me. He stops a few feet away, all cold, icy displeasure. I hate that I have to lift my chin to meet his eyes.

He flicks his gaze over my blinking Christmas bulb earrings and my red velvet dress, and as he does, a flush rolls over me, like melted chocolate poured over...okay not skin, but that's all I can think about.

Him.

Me.

Melted chocolate.

Skin.

My mouth goes dry and I send my tongue over my lips. His gaze snags on my mouth and I have a whisper of a flame flickering inside, like a candle burning in a window, just for him.

"Hello," I say, shocked at how throaty and sexy I sound. My cheeks burn as I say, "Merry Christmas."

His jaw clenches, I can actually see the muscles there tightening, and not surprisingly, the entire office goes silent.

There are thirty-two cubicles in this space. That's eight rows of four cubicles. I counted them when I strung the garland and the lights. Now, all the people in all the rows stop typing, stop moving, probably stop breathing.

It's like they're waiting for an explosion.

But why would there be one?

I was hired to decorate the offices of Cavanaugh and

Sons for Christmas. It was a rush job, booked yesterday, with a very hefty fee attached for the inconvenience. I've been here since midnight, working my behind off to make this exactly what my client asked for: the Cavanaugh offices decorated in the most magical, joyful, Christmassy way *ever*.

I'm not going to lie, it was exceedingly difficult procuring the extra supplies, finding a (nice) tree, and baking a gingerbread house all in one day. Not to mention the cookies and hot cocoa.

All in all, I'm exhausted, sore, and with the way this man is looking at me like he wants to pick me up and toss me out the window, I'm also suddenly cranky.

"What did you just say?" he asks, his voice a velvet soft warning.

Someone in a nearby cubicle gasps, the noise comes quickly then cuts off.

Goosebumps rise on my arms and I blink at the man, caught in his gaze. "Merry Christmas?"

He cocks his head, staring at me like he's trying to riddle out who I am, what I am. An alien species perhaps?

"Is this..."—he looks around the office, his lip curling—"your doing?"

I smile. Aha. He wants to thank me for doing such a splendid job. He's just gruff and...wickedly handsome. If you like that dark, icily attractive sort of look.

Which I don't.

I hold out my hand and beam at him. "Natalie Fiorre. Owner of Holiday Spirit. It's a pleasure."

He stares at my hand like it's a snake slithering out of the grass, then looks back to my smile. My cheeks are twitching though, because it's hard to hold such a bright smile while someone refuses to shake your hand or even smile back.

"I'm aware you have holiday spirit," he drawls, frowning at my flashing earrings and matching necklace. "What I'm not clear on, is why you are here, vandalizing my offices."

Oh. Okay. So he must be the other Cavanaugh. Not the nice, friendly one who hired me.

"I'm not vandalizing. That's absurd. I'm decorating. For Christmas. And let me tell you, it wasn't easy. This place was"—I clear my throat and stop before I can say "soul-destroying"—"not festive. It wasn't easy bringing all this in overnight, putting it up before the day really began. But I have, and it's made a huge difference. You can have your office party here now. Do a secret Santa, all that fun stuff. I mean..." I trail off at the growing storm crossing his face.

The furious storm pointing at me.

He takes a step forward, towers over me.

I don't back up, so I get to feel the sizzle that zings over my skin at his closeness.

Which isn't, well, it isn't right. Because I have a boyfriend. A really good boyfriend. One who is coming home with me to Romeo this Christmas to meet my family. It's a big deal. He'll be the first boyfriend I've ever brought home for the holidays.

Thus, I shouldn't be feeling zings, zaps, or goosebumps for a dark-eyed, scowling man.

He glares at me, like he can hear my thoughts.

"Take it down," he says through gritted teeth. "Take it all down. Now."

Okay, that did a good job of clearing out the zings.

"Umm. No," I say, to which he gives me a shocked look, as if no one in the entire history of the world has said no to him.

Which may be true because a woman in a nearby cubicle with sleek short hair pops her head around the divider and makes a frantic cut it out/you're dead motion.

"Did you just say no to me?" he asks. "I told you to take all this down"—he spins his finger around the office pointing at the decorations—"and you said *no*?"

Wow. This guy's a piece of work.

Everyone in this office is clearly terrified of him. Before I decorated, the place had an atmosphere like the seventh level of hell, and I don't know if he'd recognize Christmas spirit if it kicked him in the head.

So.

Somebody needs to show him that he can't intimidate people just because he's tall, handsome, and the boss.

So I give him a sugary sweet smile and say, "I'll do it again if you like. No. No. No and hmmmm, let me see...no."

Okay. So that stunned him. If I didn't know better I'd think I'd just brained him with a fireplace poker.

While he gives me an incredulous look, the sleigh bells on the break room stereo switch over to an upbeat rendition of "Jingle Bells."

That jerks him out of his shock. He leans forward, his stark black suit jacket tightening across his shoulders, and says in a quiet, controlled manner, "You will remove this...vulgar display...from my offices within the hour or I will remove it for you."

Oh.

Okay.

I don't know what to address first. The "vulgar display" jab or the removal bit.

I pull out my phone and open it, scrolling to the signed contract for my services. I hold my phone out to him, the screen showing the contract.

"I have a contract here. Full Christmas interior design services. Garland, tree, lights. Candy canes, gingerbread house, cookies, hot cocoa. Music. Christmas spirit. It's signed by the owner of this business. A binding contract between me and Gabe Cavanaugh. So, I'm sorry, but I won't be taking it down. Not today. Not until..." I look at my screen to be sure, and say, "January 2nd."

I smile at him, baring my teeth and breathing in the sweet scent of gingerbread. "So, I'll say it again. No and Merry Christmas."

He raises his eyebrows and I'm gratified to see that he's taken aback.

"Gabe Cavanaugh?" His voice is choked and disbelieving.

Uh huh.

I was mistaken before, he isn't a Cavanaugh. I'm guessing by his bad attitude that he's a midlevel manager tyrant accustomed to wielding power over his frazzled staff.

Now I've pulled out the big guns and he can't do anything about it.

"Gabe Cavanaugh hired you?"

"Yes."

"Gabe Cavanaugh signed that contract?"

"Yes," I say again, nodding happily.

At that the sleek-haired woman in the cubicle pops her head around again and makes a noooooo face, waving her arms.

I give her a reassuring smile.

It's fine.

"Since that's all taken care of," I say, "I'll just finish up here and—"

"No."

What does he mean *no*?

I sigh. "We could clear this up easily. I'll just call Mr. Cavanaugh."

He narrows his eyes. "You do that."

I scroll through my email and then hit dial on the contact number at the bottom of Gabe Cavanaugh's signature. The phone rings, rings again, and...

There's a buzzing. A vibrating. It's coming from...

The man reaches into his suit jacket pocket, pulls out a glossy black phone and hits answer.

"Yes?" he says, staring at me, his mouth tilting ironically.

I swallow, my throat full of, hmmm, is that my foot?

"May I speak with Gabe Cavanaugh?" I ask, thinking maybe he's talking to someone else, and the *yes* on my phone isn't the same *yes* that came out of his mouth.

But then, he smiles at me, a devilish, horrible smile, and says, "This is Gabe."

2

NATALIE

WHEN I WAS LITTLE I THOUGHT THAT SANTA HAD A DEVICE that let him rewind time.

That's how I reasoned out that he was able to deliver presents to all the kids in the world in one night.

Right now, I wish I had that power.

I'd rewind time to yesterday, when I got a polite, cheerful, *lovely* email from Gabe/not Gabe Cavanaugh requesting full-service rush Christmas decorations for his offices.

I'd send back—*Sorry! I'm heading up north tomorrow with my (soon-to-be fiancé) boyfriend and I don't have the time. Merry Christmas!*

Okay, I wouldn't have said exactly that, it would've been more professional, but that's the gist of it. And that would've been the end of that. I would've avoided this entire miserable morning.

I wouldn't be running on zero hours of sleep leading

up to my dinner date with Jason. The date where *he's going to propose.* All the signs are there—jumpy, nervous, questions about future plans, and talk of important discussions. We have reservations at an expensive, romantic restaurant.

So, why oh why did I take this job?

Because.

I'm a sucker for Christmas spirit.

And I thought Gabe Cavanaugh had it by the bushelful.

Turns out, that was Delilah, also known as the *Not Gabe* who sent me an email and signed a contract for my design services.

It's hard not to hear her rant while I untack yards of garland, the happy balsam scent wafting up to me. I'd offer Gabe a cookie to sweeten his temperament, but I don't think it'll work.

"Delilah. You impersonated me. Signed a binding contract using my name. What you did was illegal."

You can tell Gabe's speaking through clenched teeth. His ex-girlfriend (at least, I think she's his ex), Delilah, is on the speakerphone and you can hear her end of the conversation clear as day.

I'd tell Gabe that *everyone* can hear his conversation through his office's glass wall, all the way out here in cubicle-landia, but he doesn't like me very much. Plus I don't think he'd appreciate the interruption.

Delilah has a smoky laugh, like an old-Hollywood film star. I picture her lying on a chaise lounge, in a black silk negligee, with a long cigarette in her hand.

"Dear Gabe. Didn't you like my Christmas gift?"

"No. I did not."

She laughs again, and I adjust my picture of her to include a bob cut and vixen red lips.

Around the office, the clacking of the keyboards has quieted. Not a soul makes a peep. I don't blame them. This is juicy stuff.

I smother a yawn and then drop the last of the garland into one of my green plastic storage tubs. Maybe I'll be able to repurpose all of this. Or donate it. It'd be a shame to throw it out.

"Well," Delilah continues over the speaker phone, "my gift has served its purpose. There's nothing *you* hate more than Christmas and there is no one *I* hate more than you. I hope you choke on a candy cane."

Wow. That's some Christmas spirit.

I stand there, holding a glass jar full of candy canes as Gabe storms out of his office. He flings the door wide, and I freeze, holding the diabolical object of his fantasy demise.

His gaze flicks over me, his mouth tightening. "You're still here?"

It's been fifteen minutes. This whole office took eight hours to set up. Of course I'm still here. The jerk.

I smile brightly at him and say, "Mhmm." Then I hold out the jar and say, sweet as spun sugar, "Candy cane?"

He gives me a double-look, searching for any meaning behind my offer, but I just make my expression innocent and guileless.

Look at me, I'm a sweet, simpering, Christmas-loving fluff-brain, I wouldn't ever offer you a candy cane to choke on.

I flutter my eyelashes.

He scowls.

"Mr. Cavanaugh," a petite woman in a brown business suit with short brown hair and a nervous tremor to her voice interrupts our stand-off.

"Yes?" he says, turning away from me.

The woman seems to shrink even more as he focuses on her.

For goodness sake. What's wrong with this guy? Does he have thumb screws and medieval torture devices in his office?

"I was hoping...errr...well...Craig's Christmas play is this afternoon and I...that is...could I have a half-day today to—"

She cuts off, glances quickly at me. I shrug, hefting the jar, the candy canes clanking around, sending out sharp peppermint smells.

"You don't have any vacation time left," Gabe says, looking down at his watch.

Rude.

So rude.

"I know...but you see...it's really important..." She falters, then says pleadingly, "It's Christmas."

He shakes his head, glancing impatiently past her. "I think Craig can manage without you."

Heartless.

Terrible, horrible man.

He has to have a lump of coal for a heart. How can he

keep this woman from her son's Christmas play? It's an atrocity.

"If you'll excuse me," he says, then moves past, hurrying down the long cubicle row toward the elevator.

"I'm sorry," I whisper to the woman, sympathetic to her plight.

She looks like she's about to cry. "It's okay. I'll see it next ye-ye-"—she gives a little whimper—"year."

"There are still cookies in the break room," I tell her, nodding at where the scents of butter and sugar and ginger are trailing from. Then I have an idea. "And if you like, you can take the gingerbread house home to Craig. As a treat."

The woman steps forward, and she transforms from shaken and timid to grateful and warm. "You mean it?"

I smile, "Of course I mean it. Merry Christmas."

She hurries off with a joyful spring to her step, her brown suit pants swishing happily, humming "Jingle Bells."

I set my candy canes down in another plastic tub and then frown at the Christmas tree. It's going to take a good amount of work to get that sucker down.

Across the office the elevator dings. I glance back. Gabe's been waiting at the gray metal doors. Instead of stepping on though, he steps back.

"Mr. Cavanaugh," a man says in a robust, cheerful voice. "So glad we caught you! Merry, merry Christmas."

I open my eyes wide and turn to stare at the man who dares to spread so much good cheer.

There are three of them. They're in black top hats,

great black pea coats, and have red carnations pinned to their chests. They all have Santa beards, bushy white masses that add to the spirit.

"We won't take up your time. We're with the Christmas Club, a charity that supports—"

"No," Gabe says, attempting to step around them toward the closing elevator doors.

The speaker blocks Gabe's path, tilting his top hat toward him.

"Wait until you hear what we support. A donation from you will provide—"

"I said no. No soliciting. No badgering. No merry Christmas-ing. No thank you."

The elevator dings and before the man can say anymore, Gabe slips inside and the doors close behind him.

The man coughs into his hand in surprise and then looks around the office, like he's not quite sure what to do now.

"But it's for children," he says, looking lost.

I pull my wallet from my purse, walk over, and take out all the wrinkled bills that I have.

"Here," I say, pressing them into his hand, "Merry Christmas."

I know it's not a big donation, not like what they might have had from the owner of Cavanaugh and Sons, but it's something.

The man pats my hand, his large ones warm, and his eyes sparkling. "Thank you. Merry Christmas."

For the rest of the morning and into the afternoon, I work at undoing all the Christmas spirit in the office.

Take down the garland, the lights, the candy canes, the wreaths, the bulbs. I pass out the cookies to all the staff at their desks. It'd be a shame to waste them.

As I walk through the office, handing out cookies and candy, some of the friendlier employees chat.

"He hates Christmas. It's like this every year, all December long."

"He's a Grinch. It's miserable here in the winter."

"It's all overtime, no holiday time."

"No parties. No cookies. No cheer. Miserable."

"He even expects us to work Christmas Day."

As I un-decorate, store the finger-prickling garland, take down the pine-scented tree, click off the carols, pour out the steaming hot cocoa, I'm painting a picture of Gabe Cavanaugh.

Here's what I've discovered.

He's a humorless workaholic, bad-tempered and tyrannical, with a withered soul and a heart as wizened as a rotten apple core.

He's terrible.

Which is why I'm not surprised in the least when I learn what he's planning on doing tomorrow.

3

NATALIE

THE RESTAURANT, ALSO KNOWN AS *THE DELIGHTFULLY romantic setting where Jason will ask me to marry him*, is full of twinkling white lights, candles reflecting off crystal glassware, and the tinkling of silverware on china.

It smells like heaven—freshly made butter, baking Christmas breads with raisins, sultanas and cinnamon, honeyed ham, and yams with brown sugar.

As soon as I stepped in the restaurant, an intimate, warmly lit, rustic (but classy) bistro, all of my fatigue and frustration melted away.

Because this is it. Today is the day.

Jason was already seated at a sweet, round, white tablecloth-covered table in a little nook at the back. There were red berries mixed with evergreens in a crystal vase, glowing tea lights, and when I walked up in my red velvet dress, Jason stood and held out my chair.

Which is one of the reasons I know that we're meant to be.

He always does things like that. Pulls out my chair, holds open doors, gets out of the car first to open my door. He's a gentleman.

He works at a non-profit as their web designer, which I like. And he's tired of the dating mill, which, let's face it, we all are. He has a cat named Cookie, who he loves, which means he's actually capable of love.

He's polite. He listens.

His kisses are...okay. Ish. Okay-ish.

Fine, not to put too fine a point on it, but he has this habit of sticking his tongue in my mouth like he's a worm on the end of a fishing line and he's just wriggling around in there, searching for a trout.

It's...it's something we'll work on. Nobody's perfect. Everything else is good. Everything is great.

Well I don't know, we haven't had sex. He said he's waiting for marriage, and then he looked at me meaningfully and I was like... "Me too! Yes! Me too! Obviously, gosh. Yes. Because....yes."

Yeah. I know. I know. You shouldn't base a relationship on falsehoods. But is that really a falsehood? I'm waiting until marriage with *him*.

But suddenly I'm wondering, does kissing foreshadow sex? Will it be another worm on a hook, wriggling around all wet, flaccid, and squirmy feeling? Is that what sex will be like with him?

And do I want a lifetime of squirmy wormy wiggly sex?

Jason scrolls his phone, tapping out a quick email. His head's down, his (barely noticeable) bald spot reflecting the candlelight.

He's on call twenty-four seven; this is what happens when you're in charge of the website for a big deal non-profit. He has to check emails, take calls, fix things, during dates, while we're chatting, whenever. It's not a big deal.

Finally he looks back up, an apologetic smile on his face. "Sorry, Nat—"

He calls me Nat. I prefer Natalie, but he prefers Nat.

"Sorry. Server issue." He sets his cellphone next to his plate, then takes a sip of his red wine, sucking it through his front teeth. "You were saying?"

Right.

Jason asked me about my day when we sat down. I'd been telling him about the long night, the exhausting day, and the appalling behavior of Gabe Cavanaugh.

After lunch, I'd called my neighbor, Candace Givenchy, who works at a senior care home in the Upper East Side and she said they'd love to have the decorations.

So I transported everything over and got it all set up (with the help of their maintenance man Reginald) in time to make it, only ten minutes late, for this dinner.

And I know, *I know* I'm about to get proposed to, but I needed a minute to decompress, to destress from the day.

"You won't believe what I heard next though," I tell

Jason, leaning across the candlelit restaurant table, "Tomorrow, he's evicting families from their homes. It's unbelievable. He's tearing down a quaint five-story apartment building to make some sleek, soulless monstrosity. I bet it'll look just like his offices. Dreary, soul-sucking, heartless. He's like one of those caricature bad guys from Christmas movies. You know the ones, they're always hating on Christmas, shouting 'bah humbug,' and gleefully kicking people out of their homes on Christmas Eve."

I reach into the bread basket, grab a breadstick, and take an angry bite, chewing with relish. Then I swing it through the air, like a baton, making my point.

"If the world had any justice, then people like Gabe Cavanaugh would *actually* end up with a lump of coal in their stocking. People like him—" I fume, just thinking about his mocking smile, and take another bite of my breadstick.

"Mmm. That's good," I say. It's buttery, soft, there's a hint of rosemary and garlic. Not to be distracted though... "People like him are what's wrong with the world. Don't you think? If he just had a little less selfish spite and a little more goodwill toward men, then the world would be a better place. Right?"

Jason looks up from his phone, the blue light casting a glow on his glasses, "Sorry. What?" He looks back down, tapping at his screen.

"The world would be a better place if everyone had goodwill, a little..."

"Uh huh. Mhmm."

He's not listening. I tear another chunk of breadstick off and chew, waiting for Jason to finish his email.

In my purse, my ringtone, "Deck the Halls," goes off.

I slip it out and see *Mom* on the display. I answer, discreetly turning to the side. "Hi Mom."

"Natalie. Has he asked? Did he pop the question yet?"

I give Jason a side-glance and press the phone tighter to my ear. "Not yet," I whisper. "We're at the restaurant now."

"This is so wonderful. Remember how your father proposed to me on Christmas Day? It was a present under the tree and—"

"Yes. I know," I whisper.

Of course I know this story, we've all heard it every single Christmas, every single year, for *forever*. You'd think this story has as much weight as the actual Christmas story.

"Well. How do you look?" she asks. "Are you wearing the red dress?"

"Yes," I say.

My mom is one of the best moms alive, but she always wants me to describe everything to her in great detail, and now isn't the time.

"What did you order to eat? Is there wine? What does the restaurant—"

"Mom," I whisper, "I have to go."

"You'll call me as soon as he's asked? You'll send me a picture?"

"Yes. Bye."

"Love you!" she calls, sending a kiss, and then I disconnect.

When I turn back, Jason has put aside his phone and he's digging through the bread basket, handling all the rolls and breadsticks, pinching and crumbling them.

"So," he says, grabbing the pumpernickel roll.

"So..." I say, adding a meaningful smile. Finally, we're ready. He's going to ask the big question that he's been hinting at.

We've only been dating for two months. He hasn't met my family. I haven't even sent a picture of him to my parents or my brother (not that Felix would care). But after our first date to an obscure (and boring) foreign art film at the indie theater, we clicked.

It feels as if we've been married for fifty years.

There isn't any (inconvenient) passion, there aren't any arguments, it's like we passed all that nonsense to move right into the comfortable hand-patting, cat-on-the-lap, normal-conversations-about-the-day-without-sex-to-distract phase of life.

I have to admit, coming from Romeo, New York, soul mate capital of the world, I was a bit concerned about finding real love.

Not the Hollywood love, or the fairy-tale love, or splashy passionate love, but real love. The kind of love that can last a lifetime.

Love should be like Christmas. Kind, compassionate, loving, happy, good-willed, selfless. Like a gift that's always there. No matter what happens in life, you know without a doubt, Christmas will always come.

I always wanted a love like that. A love that, no matter what, you knew it would always be there.

I reach over and pat Jason's hand. I think this could be it.

I mean. It is it.

"So...you had a big question?" I prompt, because his eyes are drifting toward his phone again.

Like I said, I don't mind him being diligent with his job, but not while he's proposing.

"What?" He frowns. "A question?"

Then the waiter is there, setting down plates full of glazed ham and green beans with slivered almonds, and brown sugar-crusted yams.

I smile, lift up my cold metal fork, surprisingly heavy, and scoop a bit of sugary yam into my mouth.

I'm sure it's delicious, but I'm a little too nervous to enjoy it. In fact, the texture is a bit like wallpaper glue, impossible to swallow. I take a drink of my ice water.

I won't eat any more until he's asked.

"I'm really excited for you to meet my family," I tell him, smiling at the flickering candlelight reflecting off his glasses.

The restaurant speakers push out Christmas song remixes, and with the other conversations and the clatter of knives and forks against plates, it's a bit loud.

I lean closer, the tablecloth rubbing over my legs, "It's going to be wonderful. My mom and dad can't wait. Felix too. And you'll get to see Romeo. It's really romantic. I think Christmas is the best time there. And you'll see all my family's traditions—decorating and the Christmas cake, and—"

I'm getting carried away. I've never had a boyfriend home for the holidays.

In fact, when I moved to New York after college, my mom was really worried. *But how will you find your soul mate if you're not in Romeo?* she'd asked. *And how will you celebrate Christmas if you're in the city?* she'd cried.

Both were of equal importance in her mind.

Six years later, I have a solution to both. I have my own interior design company specializing in decorating businesses for the holidays. And I have a...well, a soon-to-be fiancé. A reliable, always there, comfortable guy.

"That actually leads to what I wanted to ask you," Jason says, clearing his throat and giving me an intent look.

I nod, leaning forward on my chair, the wooden edge digging into my thighs.

"Yes?"

I'm a little breathless. Dizzy. That's either due to the fact that I haven't slept in more than twenty-four hours or I'm very excited.

"I know this is fast," he says.

"Yes. Fast," I agree, nodding enthusiastically, like one of those bobbleheads on a car's dashboard.

"I mean, who would think after two months that you'd invite me to Christmas?" he shifts in his chair.

"Right. But when you know—"

"You know," he agrees.

I smile at him. Exactly.

Exactly.

I feel a glow of fondness. He's so even-tempered. He's so kind.

Unlike...my thoughts flash to Gabe and the fire he ignited inside me, and then just as quickly, I shut him out of my mind.

"Which leads me to my question."

"Yes! I will," I say quickly, then I flush, my cheeks burning, "I mean...what's your question?"

Jason taps his fingers on his phone screen and then says, "I'm going to stay in the city. You're welcome to stay too. We could catch an indie matinee on Christmas. Avoid all the hubbub. What do you think?"

Wait...

What?

Is he...is he...

Huh?

"You don't want to meet my family?"

Does this mean he's not proposing?

He shrugs. "Here's the thing, Nat. Cookie doesn't like to travel. And I can't leave her alone for more than eight hours at a time. She has generalized anxiety disorder. You know this. She needs her dad. So, I think...it's a bit more important to consider Cookie's feelings than ours. Don't you agree? That would be the Christmas thing to do."

The breadstick—which I didn't realize I'd picked up —falls from my hands and hits my ham with a squishy plunk.

He's not proposing.

He isn't...

Okay, here's what I failed to mention. When I said Jason loves his cat, what I meant was, he really, really loves his cat.

Like, his cat is his baby and he's the daddy.

There are t-shirts, and hats, and custom-made toys, and gourmet food, and also...maybe, just maybe, I might be allergic to cats.

Slightly.

As in, I sneeze every time I come near one and my eyes get so itchy I want to dig them out with a spoon.

But I've already booked an appointment with an allergist and I was going to get those shots that tone down your allergic reaction. And I've been popping allergy pills like they're candy canes on Christmas. It's fine.

Except...

"You want to stay in the city for Christmas? Because of Cookie?"

He nods, smiling at me. "You understand. I knew you would."

No.

No, I don't understand.

"You couldn't have her stay at a kennel?"

He looks at me like I just suggested sending her to the gulag with a ball gag in her little cat mouth.

"Or...a cat sitter?"

"Nat. Jeez. Do you hear yourself? Talk about soulless."

Errr. I look around the restaurant and try to regroup. I'm tired.

I'm...when I was little, there was one year, after we'd hung all the glass Christmas bulbs, that our terrier ran through the living room and knocked over the tree. All the bulbs shattered, the sound was like an explosion. I stood there, stunned, unable to think or speak for a full minute.

That is this moment.

My life has just had an explosion and the Christmas tree that I thought was my future of reliable love is now on the floor with all the ornaments shattered.

When I can finally speak, I say without thinking, "You aren't proposing?"

Jason gives me a stunned look.

Clearly, clearly the thought hadn't crossed his mind.

"Cookie doesn't like you, Nat. I wouldn't propose to someone that Cookie doesn't like. I've had doubts about even dating you. Animals know. They *know*."

A hysterical giggle wells in my chest, pushing up, trying to get out.

"Maybe I'm not exactly fond of Cookie," I say, feeling stung, thinking about the designer cat sweater I dropped two hundred dollars on as a birthday present last month.

Apparently, I shouldn't have admitted to *maybe* not liking Cookie. Jason stands, his chair legs scraping loudly on the floor.

"I liked you, Nat," Jason says in an overloud voice. "You were fun. But clearly this isn't going where either of us thought it was. If you can't show compassion for my family, a little charity and goodwill, then clearly you don't have as much Christmas spirit as you claim."

Oh no, my eyes are burning. I blink quickly. When I get embarrassed or angry, I cry. I'm not sad. Really. It doesn't hurt that I'm being dumped for a cat. I promise.

But now, all the couples at the tables around us are staring. There's even a sweet-looking old lady shaking her head at me, like I've gone and disappointed her with my uncharitable spirit.

"Goodbye, Nat. I don't think we need to see each other again."

Jason walks stiltedly from the restaurant, and apparently, out of my life.

I look down at my plate, avoiding the stares of the other diners. Ham. Green beans. Yams. I stab a green bean and shove it in my mouth, crunching down. Mmm, tastes like almonds and butter.

Well, I may as well finish, since it looks like I'm paying for the meal, and my appetite is back with a vengeance.

My mom calls twice during my meal. I send it to voicemail.

Then, as I'm scraping my fork across my plate, trying to collect the last of the sweet brown sugar yams, I realize—

This darn day isn't over yet. Because I forgot something important at Cavanaugh and Sons.

I have to go back.

4

NATALIE

I KNOW HOW IT HAPPENED.

Forgetting, not falling for a completely inappropriate man. Knowing how that happened will take copious amounts of chocolate and plenty of self-reflection.

But the forgetting, that's easy.

When I was in a rush last night, loading the van with everything for the design, I grabbed the present on accident.

I realized my mistake as soon as I brought it up to the offices. It looks almost identical to the faux, empty-wrapped presents I use for staging.

But it's not the same. It's special.

So, I put the present aside, tucking it in an empty cupboard in the break room for safe-keeping. I figured I'd grab it when I brought the thermos and cookie trays down to the truck.

I forgot it. Obviously.

"I just need to run up quickly and grab it," I tell the security guard at the entrance for the third time. "I forgot it this morning when I was taking the decorations down."

The guard stands behind a tall half-circle desk, which looks a bit like a fortress. His arms are crossed in front of him, and he shakes his head, his steel gray mustache twitching as he frowns at me.

To be honest, I'm getting a bit desperate. This present...it's special. It can't be replaced. It just...I can't ever replace it.

I hear heels sharply clicking on the marble floor in short, mincing steps. These are the steps that belong to a no-nonsense sort of person.

I turn and stare into a pair of ice-cold blue eyes. The woman, auburn-haired, gorgeous, sweeps up in a cloud of icy air and perfume that smells like violets frozen in snow.

"Is he here?" she asks, ignoring me.

The security guard shuffles and I think he's about to tip his hat. "Yes'm."

She stalks past, her heels click-click-clicking.

"Please," I say again, trying to take advantage of the guard's change in demeanor. "Mr. Cavanaugh won't mind. I just need to grab this one thing."

"Mr. Cavanaugh," the guard says in his gruff voice, "called down this morning to say you are not welcome back on the premises. Ever."

I rub my hand over my face.

Of course he did.

Heaven forbid anyone try to spread Christmas cheer.

I imagine I'm on the blacklist right next to the top-hat charity guys, Tiny Tim, and Santa Claus.

The clicking of the heels stops, the woman turns, her eyes sharp. She's elegant, really. Not the kind you get from hours at the salon and expensive clothes (although she has that), but the kind that comes from the way you move and stand.

Me, I'm too bouncy and energetic to be elegant.

"Did you say Gabe barred her from the premises?"

The guard's ears turn red and he scowls at me, like it's my fault she overheard.

"Yes'm."

She smiles then. It's a warm, inviting smile.

"Lovely." She wags her fingers at me. "I'll bring you up."

I'm not going to look this gift horse in the mouth. I hurry across the lobby, ignoring the glare of the guard.

In the elevator her icy scent wraps around me, filling the small space. Now that we're on the elevator she doesn't seem to want to chat. That's okay.

A-okay.

"Thank you," I say as the doors slide open at Cavanaugh and Sons.

The offices are back to their drab, soulless look, made worse by the darkness. The cubicles stand empty, the computer screens are black, and the only light is the emergency exit sign glowing red over the vast room.

Well, there's a light on in Gabe's office.

I can see him through the glass, his head bent over

his desk, his dark hair messy, his black suit jacket thrown over the back of his chair—but otherwise, the office is chillingly dark.

The woman ignores me, her gaze catching on Gabe like a bird dog that just spotted a downed duck in the water. She stalks toward him.

I shrug and hurry toward the break room. When there I flick on the lights. The break room is spotless again. Just a watercooler and an empty fridge. No cookies. No hot cocoa. It even smells empty and sad, like generic dish soap and dusty cupboards.

I squat down and pull open the door of the cupboard next to the sink. And yes, thank goodness, there on the bottom shelf is the present.

It's red. Silky, glossy red paper, with a beautiful, large gold bow.

I grab the present, a box, the size of a fat book, and pull it out, clasping it to my chest.

Then I notice the voices, slightly raised and...aha...I know that tone. The woman who let me in? It's Delilah.

"You have nothing to say?" she asks in that throaty, angry voice. "I return your precious ring and you have *nothing to say?*"

"I find in these instances, nothing is often the best thing to say."

I stand still, debating whether I should wait out the argument or duck behind the cubicles and try to leave unseen.

Go or stay? Go or stay?

The thought that this might end up as a make-up sex session has me leaning toward *go*.

Then there's the crash of shattering glass, and peeking around the wall, I see that Delilah has thrown a glass decanter against Gabe's office wall. It's shattered, and liquid drips down the white paint, staining it amber and gold. Glass shards litter the floor.

Delilah's chest heaves and she glares at Gabe.

Then she stalks from his office and jams her finger against the elevator button. The doors sweep open immediately, and then she's gone.

Okay.

So.

I'm just going to wait a few seconds and then I'll slowly tiptoe out of here. I clutch my present and start counting. Thirty seconds ought to do it.

One—

Two—

"What the devil are you doing here?"

5

NATALIE

GABE STANDS IN THE DOORWAY, HIS GRAY TIE PULLED loose, his shirtsleeves rolled up, his black hair a mess.

And there, on his cheek, a bright red sliver of blood where a shard of glass must have sliced him when Delilah threw the decanter.

I have a powerful urge to step forward and help patch him up. However, I squelch that urge like I'd swat a housefly circling my cookies.

It's interesting, when we spoke before, there were twinkling lights, the smell of balsam and gingerbread, and the sound of jingle bells.

I realize now that all of that was a distraction.

Because now I can smell him, and it reminds me of burying my nose in a load of freshly washed sheets, cuddling in their warmth. Not that he smells like laundry soap, he doesn't, but his clean scent, and the heat that runs over me, reminds me of lying in dryer-warmed sheets on a big, spacious bed.

Him.

Me.

Warm sheets.

It's all there. And it shouldn't be.

He hates Christmas. I love Christmas.

I just got dumped for a cat. Okay, actually, that has no relevance on my attraction to this man.

But he just got dumped by his girlfriend (fiancée?) because he's a cold-hearted wretch.

So even though he smells like a bed fantasy, and his voice—without the distraction of bells—is warm and rich like a cup of cocoa, and even though—without the distraction of twinkling lights—I find him incredibly attractive, I'm not interested.

I have what I came for, now I just need to leave.

I hold my present up. "I forgot this. I have it now. I'll just be going."

He's blocking the door, and even when I step forward, he doesn't move to the side. Instead, his dark eyebrows lower, and he stares at me like I'm a puzzle he's trying to work out.

I give a chipper smile. "Aaaand, I'll be going."

I step forward again, but he still doesn't move.

"How did you get up here?" he asks, staring at my flashing bulb earrings. I'm pretty sure he finds them atrocious.

"Your ummm...."—I wave my hand toward the elevator—"friend brought me up."

His lips twitch when I say friend, and there's a spark in his eyes like I just told the funniest joke he's ever heard.

And that spark, that little twitch of his lips has me leaning forward, wanting to see it again. It makes me think maybe he does have a heart, maybe he does just need a little Christmas spirit.

With the way he's watching me, his shoulders relaxing and his eyes laughing, he looks almost human.

Which is why I decide to stage an intervention. He can't be so terrible. Maybe no one has ever told him how he comes across? Some people just don't know that they come off as stiff, uncaring jerks.

"I'm actually glad we ran into each other," I say, trying out a smile.

He blinks, tilts his head, his shirtsleeves rustling as he crosses his arms. "You are?"

I nod, projecting confidence and positivity. "I heard while I was here today that tomorrow you're delivering eviction notices, and—"

His frown is thunderous, as if he can't fathom that I'm saying what I'm saying.

"—And I don't think you should. It's Christmastime. No one should get an eviction notice at Christmas. I don't think you're such a heartless man as to do something like that. So, I mean, you probably didn't realize that it's unkind, and now you do, and now you can...not. Do that. On Christmas."

I finish lamely, trying to keep up my bright

expression in contrast to the disbelieving scowl on Gabe's face.

"Excuse me?"

I shift on my feet and bite my lip, thinking I probably shouldn't have brought this up. Except, no one else has, have they? Or he wouldn't seem so surprised.

The refrigerator starts to hum and the noise startles me so much I jump.

Gabe sighs and shakes his head. "I see. You're one of those."

I frown. "Those?"

He sets his hand on the door jam, his fingers long and tan. "Christmas pushers. You're all the same. It's Christmas, give me money for my cause. It's Christmas, you can't expect people to pay their bills. It's Christmas, give me a bonus even though I didn't earn it. It's Christmas, give me time off even though I already used it all up. It's Christmas, say Merry Christmas back or I'll get *angry*. You Christmas pushers are all the same. You shove your cheer on everyone else, and if they don't want it, you shove it down their throats. Well, I have news for you, tomorrow, I'm hand-delivering eviction notices to all the residents of Hudson Apartments, Christmas or not."

My mouth has fallen open, my mind has turned to jelly, and the pink in his cheeks, brought on by his passionate anti-Christmas speech leaves me stunned, but more than that...

"Hudson Apartments? On West 82nd Street? That Hudson Apartments?"

The five-story building, whose bricks are tilted

diagonally so the entire place looks like a gingerbread house?

The one with the red front door and the cast-iron railing?

The one with the cracks in the plaster and the squeaky stairs, and the banister that's just a little loose?

Surely not that Hudson Apartments.

Gabe narrows his eyes. "What do you know about it? Are you with the co-op board?"

Oh no.

He does mean that Hudson Apartments.

And those families that are getting evicted? Those are my neighbors. Mrs. Givenchy and her two miniature poodles, Gracie and Mannie. The Lawsons and their two little girls. The Tsangs, who are enjoying their retirement after forty years working for the MTA. More. Five floors more.

I shake my head, grip my present to my chest, my heart rattling in my ears.

"But...but...that's *my* home."

Then Gabe says exactly what I should've come to expect from a man with a rotten apple core for a heart.

"Then I suppose when you get your eviction notice, it won't come as a surprise."

6

GABE

I brush the shattered glass into the dustpan, the tinkling music of the shards the only noise in the silent office.

I kneel close to the floor, the smell of peat and smoke rising from the amber stain spreading over the gray carpet. The whiskey smell is almost strong enough to block out the lingering scent of gingerbread, peppermint, and evergreen.

Unfortunately, whiskey isn't strong enough to block out Christmas.

That's a known fact.

I grip the cool plastic dustpan, now full of glistening glass shards, reminiscent of icicles striking concrete, and let them slide, flashing and jingling into the trash.

The light reflecting off the glass, playing in golds and reds and silvers, reminds me of the woman.

What was her name again?

The light played off her in the same way, her necklace and earrings flashing unapologetically.

When I stepped off the elevator this morning, I didn't see the decorations—not at first.

I'd been reading an email, formulating a reply, expecting my office to remain that cool, monotone haven, a refuge from the annual Christmas assault that takes over the city.

Then I heard it. The sound of bells, high and bright and annoyingly cheerful.

And then the smell of gingerbread and evergreen grabbed me by the throat and squeezed.

I looked up quickly, dumbfounded that somehow Christmas had retrenched and my office was the new frontline. But instead of seeing the office strung up with garish decorations and the giant Christmas tree, I saw her.

The long rows of cubicles, the overhead fluorescent lights, the gray walls, the gray carpet squares, all of it became a sort of M.C. Escher painting arrowing dizzily to her.

The entire office was bathed in grayscale, the rows narrowing and pointing, all leading to the one bright, shining woman.

I'd never seen her before. If I had I would've dropped down on my knees and proposed the second I laid eyes on her.

She was the only spot of color in the whole world.

She was glowing and bright, her face lit with a carefree, joyful smile that lifted me up just from being near.

Her hair was a mass of chestnut curls, long and wild, and my fingers itched to bury in its softness and kiss her. Because her mouth, it was bright red and laughing.

I took a step forward, moving without thought. I was in a stupor, a haze, my heart tugged me forward and I followed. I didn't know who she was, but I knew it was fate that she was here. She...she...she was glowing because of the red and green Christmas lights flashing at her ears.

I jerked to a stop, shook my head. My shoulders tightened as I breathed in the gingerbread scent filling the office.

The woman was bright because she was in a red velvet Christmas dress. She was laughing because she was surrounded by a mountain of garland, a river of blinking lights, a choir of jangling Christmas chords.

No.

A tight fist closed around my heart and a bitter, metallic tang burned my throat.

Behind me, the elevator doors dinged shut, a brush of air pushing over me.

All of that, finding the woman of my dreams and then losing her to Christmas took less than five seconds.

My life changed, I found her, needed her, wanted her, and then the door slammed shut.

It's then I took in the rest of my office. The cool, quiet space that kept the season out had been transformed from a professional workspace to a Christmas fantasyland.

My stomach rolled, my throat burned. The sound of jingle bells struck me like the hooves of the horse on that darned sleigh kicking me in the head.

It was all her fault.

The woman who I thought was the one was not. She was, in reality, everything that I loathed, come to stick a sharpened candy cane in my heart and twist.

Let's just say I didn't respond well when confronted with that fact.

She took her Christmas and herself away and if there's a dull emptiness in me, well that's just December, isn't it?

It's nothing that hasn't happened before and won't happen again next year.

I drop the dustpan next to the trash bin and stride over to my desk.

My office is along the eastern side of the building, a wall of windows looks over the city and a sea of windows looks back, hundreds of offices, thousands of lives. It's dark, but I'm not the only one with my lights on, working. Seeing the yellow lights dotting other office buildings makes me feel less alone.

I sit in the cold leather chair, run my hands over the cool walnut of my desk, and close my eyes, feeling the dry heat of the HVAC humming overhead. The spilled whiskey scent is so strong I can taste it.

I reach down to the bottom drawer of my desk, slide it open and pull out an orange prescription bottle.

The pills clank and rattle as I set the bottle on my desk. I stare at it. Drum my fingers against my desk.

My computer screen turns on from the vibration, bathing the dimly lit room in a blue artificial glow. My bookshelves across the room, the modern paintings on the wall from the gallery down the street, the leather chair facing my desk, they all turn computer blue.

The ringing of my phone jars the silence. It's my cell, otherwise I'd let it go to voicemail. I smile when I see who it is.

"What do you want?" I say, leaning back in my chair.

"Good question. Hello Gabe," says Cecily, her Long Island accent strong, which means she's irritated with me. Whenever she's prickly her accent comes on hard. "Since you asked, I'd like a trip to Barbados, all expenses paid, with an all-day kids club for June and Jeb so I can wear a bikini, lounge by the pool, drink a liter of strawberry daiquiris, and have some uninterrupted alone time with Dale. How's that sound?"

I lean forward, my chair squeaking, and drop my elbows to my desk.

"Hi Cecily."

She huffs. I can feel her displeasure over the phone. She's my cousin, two years older than me, a nurse at a hospital in Long Island, and mom to my niece and nephew.

As kids, we spent most summer vacations together, wandering the hot sidewalks of the city, eating sticky melting popsicles, and splashing each other in public fountains.

She knows I don't do December, or Christmas, which is why she's calling.

"Hi Gabe. You haven't been by in weeks."

"Yes." That's not unusual. I don't ever come by in December.

"The kids miss you."

"They miss me giving in and buying them whatever they want," I say, flicking my finger against the orange pill bottle. The pills rattle and clank against the plastic.

"Are you still at the office?" she asks, a frown in her voice.

"I'm working on the Hudson Apartments," I tell her, thinking about how the woman came back, how she told me she lives there.

I shift uncomfortably, ignoring the ghost of gingerbread and peppermint.

"I don't like that project," Cecily says. She's voiced concerns since the beginning.

"I know. Neither do I." We're silent for a moment, then I say, "Delilah stopped by."

Cecily and Delilah were once friends, which is how Delilah and I met.

"I'm sorry. Did she throw something?"

Delilah is known for throwing things when she wants to make a point. She was a stellar dodgeball player in high school.

"She did. I ended our…" I don't know what to call it.

"Booty calls?"

"It was never—"

"I don't actually want to know."

"Regardless. I told her we wouldn't be seeing each other anymore."

"Good. She's not right for you."

I smile. Cecily doesn't hold back.

We're quiet for a moment. On my end there's the hum of the air vent, the flutter of a piece of paper on the desk in the cross breeze of the air, and the static flicker of my screen.

On her end there's the sound of dishes being loaded into a dishwasher, running water, and the kids' voices, barely distinguishable.

She's surrounded by family, doing the dishes, hearing their warmth. She'll have her tree up, a wreath on the door, presents under the tree.

Me? I'm here, surrounded by silence. Alone.

"I called to ask you over for Christmas dinner," she says, her voice falsely casual. "Eight o'clock at our place, no need to bring anything."

I pause and consciously keep my jaw from tightening, "I'll think about it."

"You say that every year."

"And I think about it every year." I think about it for the second it takes me to discard it.

She sighs, "Gabe. You can't keep doing this. Shutting out Christmas won't bring Lee back."

My chest tightens, that fist around my heart clenching. I shove my chair back and stand, pacing to the window.

The city lights are bright, far down below a bell ringer jangles their bell for Christmas charity. They aren't having any luck, the snow-covered sidewalks are nearly empty of people.

When I don't answer her, Cecily continues, her voice insistent, "Every year it's the same. You close yourself off. You refuse to acknowledge Christmas. It's not right. Lee loved Christmas. You can't keep shutting yourself off. Lee would want—"

"You have no idea what Lee would or wouldn't want. This has nothing to do with Christmas. It has nothing to do with Lee."

Cecily gives a sharp huff. "Fine. We'll not talk about it. The invitation stands. Christmas dinner. The kids miss you."

After Cecily hangs up I stand at the window, ignoring the blurry line of my reflection. I know what I'd see. A hard mouth, exhaustion, the weight of Christmas past pushing down on me.

Cecily has a picture of us, Lee and I, holding hands standing next to Cecily, grinning in front of the Rockefeller Christmas tree. She told me she puts it out every Christmas. I saw it the one and only time I went to her place in December. After that, I've never been back.

I turn and stride to my desk, grab the bottle of pills.

I twist the cap, the edges scraping my palm as I pull it free. The lid lifts with a pop. The pills have a chemical coating smell.

I didn't expect to need this.

But the exhaustion is too much. I'm buried in it. And the woman from earlier? The one who I thought was color in all the grayscale? She was as false as Christmas cheer.

The scent of whiskey hits me again, and below that the mean pull of balsam and Christmas cookies.

What does it matter?

Screw it.

7

NATALIE

I HIT MY HEAD AGAINST MY STEERING WHEEL, THUNKING IT again and again.

Dumped for a cat. Thunk. Evicted by a scrooge. Thunk. Merry freaking Christmas. Thunk.

My car, a decades old, canary yellow Ford is so cold the steering wheel is like an ice chunk and the vinyl seats are like ice cubes.

The engine is on, coughing phlegmatically in the winter cold, but it takes a good twenty minutes for the engine to stop wheezing and hacking and start heating.

I let out a sigh and a cloud of winter mist hangs in front of me. I shiver and rub my gloved hands over my arms. I'm in my snowflake scarf, my fluffy boots, and my puffy coat, but it's going to be a bit before I'll feel even remotely warm.

My windshield is covered in a thin layer of frost. The LED Christmas lights hanging from my rearview mirror flash, and the red and green lights flickering in the cold confines of my car are like a portent of trouble to come.

This part of Midtown is quiet. The only noises I hear outside of my frosted, grumbling car are the snowplows scraping the streets and the salt trucks rumbling past.

It's a light snow, it won't be more than two inches, and right now the flakes fall fat and light, like angels' feathers floating down from heaven.

But all the same, the night and the snow have driven most people inside. Back to their homes to have mulled cider, or hot cocoa, and cuddle on the couch with a book and a blanket.

Thinking of home makes my gut clench, a panicky, desperate sort of feeling. Tomorrow all of my neighbors are going to receive the worst Christmas present ever.

I think about Maria and Daryl Lawson. They have two girls, Felicity who is eight and Bianca who is four. This past year, Bianca was in and out of the hospital; she had pediatric heart surgery. I helped Maria decorate their apartment, so that Bianca could have the best Christmas ever.

At home.

If Gabe Cavanaugh delivers those notices it won't be the best Christmas ever. Not even close. The Lawsons deserve a happy Christmas.

So does Mrs. Givenchy.

She spends every day taking care of others and then she comes home and does little things for her neighbors —dropping off cookies, picking up their newspaper, delivering homemade soup if she hears they're sick. Her husband died five years ago, at seventy-one, and she says what keeps her going is her work and the family she's made in our building.

The Tsangs, they are the kindest couple I know. They plant flowers in the building's window boxes in the spring, summer, and fall, and in the winter Mr. Tsang delivers poinsettias to every home in the building.

I've lived in my building for six years, ever since I graduated from college, got myself a job as an interior designer at a furniture store, and then saved, saved, saved until I could start my own business.

It's my home.

I sniff, my nose numb from the cold. My car smells like gingerbread and ice. I'd usually find the smell comforting, but now it reminds me of Gabe, and it just makes me feel helpless, powerless.

There's nothing I can do to help my friends.

Nothing.

And tomorrow, I was supposed to drive up to Romeo with my fiancé to spend a joyful Christmas with my family.

When they find out I was very wrong about Jason's *big question,* my brother Felix will laugh, my dad will grunt and say Jason wasn't good enough for me, and my mom will get a worried expression and say, *why don't you move back to Romeo, where you'll be sure to find your soul mate?*

The thing is, I don't want to move back to Romeo. I like my home (sob). I like my business. I've worked hard.

It's successful. People love what I do. I'm good at it. And isn't it possible that I might find true love here?

My phone rings, "Deck the Halls" blaring loudly in my car. I tug it out of my purse, expecting my mom. Instead it's an unknown number, but the area code is for Romeo.

"Hello?"

There's Christmas music on the other end and lots of voices.

"Who is this?" a woman with a very familiar voice asks. "Hello? Hello?"

"Hello? I'm here. Miss Erma, is that you?"

I swear it is. Miss Erma is famous in Romeo. She's the reason my parents are married, thus she's the reason I exist. I'm pretty grateful to her for that.

The rest of the town is grateful too, considering she's matched about eleventy-thousand people with their soul mate. Miss Erma is the major reason my mom keeps asking me to come home. Because if I'm not near Miss Erma, how will she see my soul mate?

Mom logic.

Miss Erma makes a humph noise and says, "Of course it's me. Who else would it be? I call you every week."

Errr. No. "Umm, Miss Erma? This is Natalie Fiorre."

I haven't actually spoken to Miss Erma since last year's Christmas Parade. She asked me if I'd made the mistletoe earrings I was wearing (I had).

The snowplow rumbles by again, scraping the pavement and making my car shake and vibrate as it rolls past. My car is moving from its wheezing, freezing stage to its nearly warm but not quite stage.

"Natalie! I didn't know you started working at the pizza parlor. I thought you were an interior designer." Then before I can respond, Miss Erma says loudly, "Wanda, you won't believe it, Natalie's working at Romeo Pizza now! Who's Natalie? Natalie Fiorre! Jerry and Roberta's daughter, the curly-haired one that went to New York to be a designer. Well I don't know why she's working at the pizza place, you'll have to ask her—"

"Miss Erma, I'm not..." I pinch the space between my eyebrows and shake my head. "I'm not working at the pizza parlor."

"Well why are you answering their phone then?"

"Umm. I answered my phone. You called me."

"No. I called Romeo Pizza and you answered. Hang on, Wanda, I'm getting to it. Okay. Natalie, I know you're new, so I'll go slow. Wanda wants a thin crust, no sauce, extra cheese, pineapple on one quarter, green peppers on one quarter, and sausage on the other half. And I want a thick crust, extra sauce, cheese, feta, olives, and bacon...oh wait, not bacon, Wanda says I'll like the chipotle sausage. Is that chipotle sausage any good?"

I blink, holding my phone to my ear, and shake my head. "I...I have no idea. I guess it would be?"

"Hmm. You should learn the toppings if you're going to work at the pizza place."

"But...I'm not. I'm Natalie. I'm not Romeo Pizza. This isn't their number."

The music is loud on her end, and as I speak, there's a cheer.

"What did you say?" Miss Erma asks. "It's our holiday party tonight. It's a great time, but the food is terrible. Lucky for us, we have you."

Okay.

Got it.

I'm going to have to call Romeo Pizza and put in Miss Erma and Wanda's order.

The frost on my windshield is thawing, the ice melting, leaving clear glass behind. The air is less ice and more gingerbread, and my nose isn't quite so numb.

I can drive home now, get some sleep, head to Romeo in the morning. Figure things out.

But...I have Miss Erma on the line.

She's smart. She's wise.

"Miss Erma, I have a question."

"Yes, dear?"

"I met someone today. He hates Christmas. He broke his ex-girlfriend's heart, he turned away charity, he makes his employees work overtime on Christmas day, he called my decorations a vulgar display, he's the epitome of a modern Scrooge. And tomorrow he's delivering eviction notices to everyone in my building. And I was wondering...what I should do?"

"Do?" asks Miss Erma.

"Yes," I say, gripping my phone tightly, "What should I do?"

"Hmm. What's his name?"

"Gabe Cavanaugh," I say, his name as soft as a snowflake melting on my tongue.

"I suppose what you should do is bring him home for Christmas."

I blink, shocked, the still cold vinyl seat pressing against my thighs. "Sorry?"

"Isn't that what happened to Scrooge? The ghosts dragged him around, making him see the error of his ways? Well, drag him around. Give him some Christmas spirit. That'll fix everything."

"Christmas spirit?"

"Mhmm."

I shake my head, trying to think about what Miss Erma is recommending. "Are you saying I should force him to experience Christmas?"

"Did I say that? Hmm. Well, I'm sure an opportunity will fall into your lap. Like a Christmas present appearing under the tree! What's that, Wanda? Oh, Natalie, Wanda says she wants an order of garlic knots too. How long will it be until our pizza gets here?"

I frown, "Umm. Forty-five minutes?"

"Perfect. Good luck," Miss Erma says, her voice warm, "and good luck with your new job. Merry Christmas!"

"Merry Christmas," I say automatically, and then Miss Erma is gone.

I smile to myself, the quiet of the car surrounding me, then I look up Romeo Pizza's number and phone in Miss Erma's order.

After I'm done, my car is warm, my steering wheel is

no longer an icicle, and the road has been plowed and salted. I can head home.

I'll crawl into my bed and sleep the night away. Then rested, I'll head up to Romeo.

But forcing Gabe Cavanaugh to experience Christmas cheer?

That's not gonna happen.

While Miss Erma may know a lot about soul mates, I guess she doesn't know as much about scrooges.

I highly doubt that some candy canes and mistletoe are going to thaw his heart.

I shift my car into drive and put my turn signal on. As I'm about to pull out, there's a forceful, impatient knock on my passenger door.

It's Gabe Cavanaugh.

8

HE'S BUNDLED IN A BLACK WOOL COAT, A GRAY SCARF, AND wearing his usual forbidding expression. His gloved fist knocks again against my back passenger seat, snowflakes swirling around him.

"Taxi," he says in that commanding way he has. Then he tugs on the door handle.

"Oh for the love of—" I shake my head.

Okay, so this happens sometimes. I drive a yellow sedan. I also live in New York City, where yellow sedans are typically taxis.

However, my yellow sedan is *canary* yellow, and taxis are—for lack of a better word—*taxi* yellow. With large black block letters stating NYC Taxi on their side. And they, you know, have a glowing placard on top of their car.

However, sometimes, a person gets it into their head

that I'm a taxi. And then they want a ride. They don't get a ride.

I could get another car, but this one gets great gas mileage, fits into the smallest street parking spots, and is dinged up enough that I don't mind when it gets nicks and scratches in the street parking melee. It's a good city car. Except for the occasional taxi mix-up, of course.

"Not a taxi," I call. Loudly.

Gabe knocks again, his breath puffing around him. He rubs his hands on his arms like he's cold, then looks up and down the quiet, dark street.

There aren't any taxis. There aren't really any cars unless you count the snowplows and salt trucks. It's a quiet, snowy night.

Gosh, he's not going away. Of course he's not going away. He's stubborn and tyrannical and intimidates people into doing what he wants.

I unlock my doors. I'm going to have to get out and tell him what's what.

But before I can, Gabe flings open the unlocked door and slides into the back seat.

"Houston and Wooster," he says.

I quirk my eyebrow, then turn to look.

His presence has filled my car, the heat of him, the energy of him, the zing and magnetism, even that delicious *bed* scent.

I wrinkle my nose.

"Look, Gabe. I'm not a taxi. What's..." I trail off, grip my seatback, and stare at him.

His head lolls to the side, his mouth falls slightly open, and his eyes are closed. He lets out a soft snore.

A snore.

He's asleep?

In my car?

Asleep, after ten seconds? Who is this man?

"Hey. Gabe. Mr. Cavanaugh. Wake up!"

He doesn't.

I scowl at him. He looks all cute, and soft, and I can imagine running my hands over the stubble at his jaw. Ugh.

"Wake up!" I shout.

He doesn't.

That is some champion sleep going on.

I thrust open my door, climb out into the freezing cold, the snowflakes flying, and crunch over the ice and salt.

I yank open the back seat door and then grab his shoulder. He's warm, his shoulder is muscled and firm. I shake him. Hard.

"Gabe. Wake up. I'm not a taxi."

"Mmmm," he says, his eyelids fluttering. Then he brushes my arm off and buries his head in his sleeve.

What in the world. What in the ever-loving—

Wait.

Didn't Scrooge fall asleep before Marley's ghost came? Didn't he nod off and then *poof* Marley was there?

This isn't a normal sleep. This is more like a magical sleep. And if that's the case, then Miss Erma isn't just a soul mate seer, she's a Christmas spirit prognosticator!

Gabe Cavanaugh fell into my lap, just like she said he would.

Which means...

I have to force him to experience Christmas joy.

I have to make him see the error of his ways.

And the only way I can do that is by doing exactly as Erma said.

Bring Gabe to Romeo, she said.

Make Gabe experience Christmas, she said.

That will fix *everything*, she said.

So I shut the back door. I climb into the front seat. I pull my car onto the road and then I drive, slowly, carefully, onto the highway north.

Sixty miles in, Gabe stirs, mumbling, turning restlessly.

So, I do what Marley's ghost would do, I pull off on a deserted road, quiet with snow covering the tops of pine trees, a deer peeking at me from the woods, and I drag Gabe from the car.

He's heavy, solid with muscle. That's okay, I'm strong from hauling Christmas trees, garland, and tubs full of decorating supplies.

I pocket his phone and his wallet for good measure, then I bind his legs and hands with Christmas lights and foist him into the trunk.

After I close the lid—having only dropped him once —the deer stares at me, chewing the bark from a tree.

"What?" I say. "He could wake up and make a ruckus. He'll be angry. Enraged even. He could force me off the road, or...this is better. Plus, he might sleep the whole way there. Magic sleep. He'll never know. He'll wake up at the cabin, all ready for Christmas cheer."

The deer isn't impressed. The snowflakes falling from the star-studded sky aren't impressed. The quiet whistle of wind through snow-covered trees is not impressed.

Some—okay most—might say this is kidnapping.

I shy away from that word. It sounds devious. Criminal. Wrong.

There's nothing wrong about what I'm doing.

I'm saving my friends from Christmas eviction.

I'm saving Gabe from a lifetime of wizened heart misery.

I'm saving Christmas.

So, we won't say Gabe's been kidnapped.

We'll say he's been...scrooged.

9

NATALIE

I PULL SLOWLY DOWN THE LONG DRIVEWAY LEADING TO MY family's cabin.

The evergreens lining the drive stand tall, like nutcrackers wearing hats of snow, nodding as I pass.

The woods are thick and quiet, with slim dogwood branches sticking up from the wind-carved snowbanks.

I know, during the day, the dogwood branches will be a bright ruby red, vibrant against the white snow. And the snow will be sloped and swirled from all the wind whipping down the tree tunnel driveway leading to the cabin.

There aren't any lights on at the cabin. In fact, the only light is the moon glistening off the snow and my headlights cutting through the dark.

My tires crunch over the snow on the—blessedly plowed—driveway. But I still drive slowly. The last thing

I need is careening into the ditch while I'm scrooging Gabe.

My radio crackles, starting to lose the signal on the Christmas radio station I found. It's one of those twenty-four seven deals, where it's Christmas songs from Thanksgiving until the New Year. "Silent Night" cuts in and out, the singer's voice warbling with static.

The loss of signal is because I'm in the middle of nowhere.

Sure, Romeo is twenty miles away, but that twenty miles is full of thick forests, marshes, mountains, caves, and so much no-man's land that once you pass over the mountain and descend into the snow-covered valley, you wouldn't know civilization was anywhere to be found.

My parents bought the cabin twenty-five years ago as a retreat. Summer hiking. Autumn bonfires. Winter cross-country skiing.

My family also comes out here every year from Boxing Day until New Year's Day. Which means...the drive is kept plowed, the cabin is likely clean-ish, and of course, it's empty.

Empty for four more days.

The cabin rises out of the snow, its roof covered with a layer of white, icicles lining the roofline, like frosting from a gingerbread house.

The cabin is square, the round brown logs that construct it give it a homey, rustic look. The windows are wide and the sills are lined with snow. A warm, happy feeling rushes over me.

I love this cabin. I can already smell the smoke from

the fire, hear the crackle of the logs, and taste the homemade hot cocoa mix my mom keeps in the pantry. This place is a haven.

Now that I've seen it, there isn't a doubt in my mind that it's going to transform Gabe. No one can stay in the Fiorre family cabin, outside Romeo New York, and not feel the good in the world.

With that thought, I pull to a stop, put the car in park, and then turn off the engine. The stereo keeps playing, the music loud as I strain to hear...anything.

Is he awake?

Is he moving?

Was that a noise?

But no. I don't hear anything but the chords of "Silent Night."

So I take a breath, give myself a pep talk—you can do this, Miss Erma predicted this, you are saving Christmas—and then step out of my car.

The door hinges squeak loudly in the quiet. I slam it shut and the noise echoes off the snow and the ice.

The wind lets out a soft sigh, rustling the trees. The snowflakes, as small as stardust, float around me, lighting on my cheeks and nose, leaving cold little winter kisses.

I shiver. There isn't any noise coming from the trunk.

The snow crunches beneath my feet as I walk around my car.

I stop in front of the trunk. I stand there, my insides twisting, my heart thumping, my breath rising in front of me, and then...I fling the trunk open.

10

NATALIE

HE BURSTS OUT OF THE TRUNK, HIS EYES GLOWING IN THE moonlight, a snarl on his lips.

I dodge to the side and he rolls past me, hitting the ground violently.

The snow lets out a crunch, a groan, and then he's rolling, kicking across the ice, and slamming into the snow bank.

I stare at him, my breath short, my heart pounding, as he army crawls over the snowbank, powdered snow flying around him.

Okay, so I was right. When he woke up he was likely...upset.

Very, very...upset.

Okay, fine. He's enraged.

But what do I know? That could be his default status. So far, I've only seen cold, rude, and enraged. So.

He hits a soft spot in the snowbank then, probably

carved out by the wind, and it gives way under his weight. The snow groans, and he's rolling again, falling face first into the powder.

I step forward, the cold biting at my nose, nipping at my hands.

I didn't put my coat back on after shedding it once my car heated up. I'm just in my velvet dress, scarf and boots, with only my flashing earrings and necklace to keep me warm.

I take another step forward, the silver light of the moon spilling over us.

Gabe is straining at the Christmas lights binding him. It looks like he's trying to snap them free with sheer strength. Or sheer outrage.

Suddenly he flips over, a snarl on his face, his eyes glowing like two black coals. His face is covered in snow, his midnight black hair full of snowflakes. His cheeks are red and when he sees me his lips form a sneer.

"You," he says, and his voice hits me like a cold arctic blast.

I put my hands on my hips and let him look his fill. He takes in my wildly curling hair, my earrings spilling red and green light over the snow, my red velvet dress hugging my curves.

His gaze rakes over me, like warm fingers dragging over cold skin. I was icy from the winter wind, but suddenly I'm flushed and hot.

He stares me down and says in that deep voice that makes me shiver, "You are going to rot in prison for a very, very, very long time."

I can't help it, I laugh. It bursts from me, low and husky, and his eyes flare with astonishment.

What if I do? What if he's right? Well, I'm here now aren't I?

I've done it. I'm in up to my chin in this.

I'm scrooging Gabe Cavanaugh.

And the only thing to do when you're on a one-way road?

Keep going.

Full steam ahead.

It's time for some Christmas cheer.

I purse my lips, wink, and say cheerfully, "Ho, ho, ho, Scrooge. And a Merry Christmas to you too."

11

GABE

I'VE BEEN KIDNAPPED BY A CHRISTMAS CUCKOO, A FESTIVE fanatic, a noel nutcase.

She's some sort of deranged madwoman and somehow I've fallen into her crazed Christmas delusions.

Earlier today she seemed normal. At first, she seemed stunningly *perfect*.

Granted, she wrapped my office in hundreds of yards of tinsel and flashy lights, but she thought she'd been hired. Simple mistake. Easily rectified.

Then, when she came back and gave me a piece of her mind about the Hudson project, I gave her leeway because she lives there.

But this? This?

She shoved me in her trunk and drove me to...

I look around, once again taking in the thick pine and cedar woods, the deep snow, the brilliantly clear and *starry* night. One thing is for certain, we are nowhere near Manhattan.

The cold snow is now in my shoes, stinging my hands and ankles, even my face. The cedar scent is sharp, and the woman is smiling at me as if we are *friends*.

There's only one thing to do. I spring up. She takes a quick step back.

Good. Be afraid.

Then I jerk my legs, kick so that the lights loosen enough for me to half-run, half-limp down the drive.

I might look like a wounded antelope running from a cheetah, but I'm moving.

If I can make it to the road, I'll signal a passing motorist for help. Then I'll call the police.

"Hey!" she cries, her voice loud and echoing, "Where are you going?"

I don't look back. The more I run, the looser the lights around my legs become.

Pins and needles sensations are piercing my calves and feet. They'd fallen asleep, but the blood is moving again.

I hear the crunch of her footsteps over snow as she runs after me.

I ignore her, tugging at my wrists. There's more circulation in my hands. The tang of blood on my lips mixes with the cedar and ice. I wonder, did she hit me? Knock me out?

Then suddenly, I remember.

The taxi—she was the driver. I climbed in, then...oh.

The sleeping pills I took, the ones my doctor recommended (take an hour before bed), and that I'd been holding off on trying? Apparently, they hit me like a sledgehammer.

I won't be taking those again. I like to sleep, but I don't like to sleep so well that I can be shoved in a trunk by a five-foot-six woman and carted out of the city.

"Hey," she says again, catching up to me, "What are you doing?"

I glare down at her, pink cheeks, curly hair framed with snow, gorgeous really. Gorgeous but demented.

"Escaping," I growl. "What does it look like?"

In fact, the Christmas lights have almost unwound from my legs.

"No. You can't."

No? What is it with this woman and telling me no?

"I can. I am."

"No. You can't. We're more than twenty miles from the nearest house. This road is an old logging road, no one uses it. It's ten degrees out. You try to escape, you die. Hey stop!"

I've picked up the pace, the Christmas lights have nearly unraveled.

But then, she does something unexpected.

She pumps her arms, darts toward me, and hits me with her shoulder below my center of gravity.

My momentum, the way she hits me, it all has me flying through the air and rolling headfirst into the snow.

But then, she's falling too. We go down in a tangle of legs and arms and Christmas lights.

I land in the snow, the cold powder catching me, and then she crashes on top of me. My breath whooshes out and my lungs seize, leaving me struggling for breath.

She isn't much better. She shakes her head, coughs, then presses her hands into my chest.

"Ohhhh," she groans. "That went a little different than I envisioned."

Finally I manage to pull in a breath.

With her this close I can taste gingerbread and frosting. And now, with my hands tied between us and the rest of her pressed into me, I can feel every inch of her.

She's warm, she's curvy, her hips are nestled between my legs, and there's that feeling again. The one from when I first saw her. It's as if every cell in me is lit up, burning as bright as the Rockefeller Center Christmas tree.

As soon as I saw her it was as if the lights that have been off for years were flipped on. Everything in me glows. As if she has all the electricity I need to power this feeling.

Too bad she's a maniac.

I shift under her, wondering if I should just dump her off me into the snow. Icy flakes are creeping down my collar, sending cold down my neck.

She's staring at me, a bemused expression on her face. "Did you know your lip is bloody?"

I lift an eyebrow. "These things happen when you kidnap someone."

Her eyes light with surprise. "Oh no. No." She shakes her head. "I didn't kidnap you. I scrooged you."

I stare, the snow falls around her, the wind rustles her hair, her sweet sugary scent falls over me. "Excuse me?"

She smiles at me. "You got into my car. Then you passed out. And I would've taken you home, but I talked to Miss Erma and she said—"

"Who is Miss Erma?" I ask, wondering if Miss Erma is some crime boss with a penchant for kidnapping men.

"Oh she's a soul mate psychic. She's famous. Anyway, she called and told me I had to take you home. I had to force you to experience Christmas. She said that would fix *everything*. Then she said you'd just fall in my lap. And you did. So I brought you home and now you are going to stay here until Christmas, doing Christmassy things...I..." She frowns at me, her red lips bright as winter berries. "I haven't figured out what yet, but I will. All I know is that just like Scrooge, you need a huge dose of Christmas and I'm going to give it to you."

She smiles then, and a chill rolls down my spine, like an icy finger dragging an icicle over my skin.

"I won't," I say. "I loathe Christmas."

She nods. "I know. You're a scrooge. But come December 26th, you'll be back in New York, back to your life, and all this will be over—"

"Like the nightmare it is—"

"And I'll—"

"Be in prison—"

"Be with my family, enjoying Boxing Day and then New Year's, and everything—"

"Will be over for you because you're a deranged criminal—"

"Will be perfect. Because you'll see that there isn't anything that a little Christmas spirit can't fix—"

"Except criminal charges and prison time."

She grins at me and wiggles a bit, and that wiggling, it has my body lighting up, my blood warming again, and my hands aching to be free of this Christmas cord so that I can...nothing.

Except...did she say all this would be over by December 26th?

"I'll be back in the city on Boxing Day?" I ask, looking carefully at her expression.

"Of course."

"You'll take me back to the city?"

"Ye-es." She frowns at me, her eyebrows lowering, and the soft velvet of her dress rubs over my hands.

"That's not soon enough. Give me the car keys," I say in a hard demanding voice.

She raises her eyebrows, unfazed. "No."

No? Again?

"I can force you."

I could easily overpower her, take the keys, leave her here to wait for the police to come cart her away. She could have a nice Christmas dinner behind bars.

"No you can't."

"Why not?"

She smiles, triumph in her expression, "Because I

threw the car keys in the woods. They're buried somewhere in a snowbank. Lost for all eternity. Or until spring thaw."

I stare at her, speechless. "Why would you do that?"

She wrinkles her nose. "Insurance. Besides, I'll have my parents bring the spare keys when we're ready to leave."

This woman has parents? People who love her and bring her things like spare car keys? Mind-boggling.

I decide to change tactics.

"We're in the middle of nowhere? There isn't any way to leave this cabin without freezing to death?" My nose is an icicle, my ears two little pained ice blocks, already I'm feeling the ten-degree chill to the bone.

"Exactly," she says. "You have to stay. Trust me."

Right. I trust her less than I trust a pickpocket in Times Square.

But slowly I nod, the snow scraping along the back of my neck.

"You'll have fun," she says, "Think of it as a vacation. A retreat. An all-inclusive Christmas package."

I think I have a clear picture of what's going on. This nutty woman thinks she can Christmas me into not evicting her, or letting her decorate my offices, or some other wacky idea she's clinging to. She's a criminal, but I don't think she's dangerous.

All I have to do is watch and wait, and soon enough I'll find an opportunity to escape. Somehow.

Because days of Christmas spirit? That's my worst nightmare.

But for now, I'll play along.

"Okay," I say, trying on a smile for her benefit. My mouth curves upward, and the cold bites at my lips.

She gives me a stunned look, blinking quickly, then she shakes her head. "Okay? Okay, okay?"

I nod. "Sure. Okay. I trust you."

She smiles then, and the wattage of it kicks me in the chest, robbing me of breath.

Before I breathe again she crawls off me, wiping the snow from her dress in a misty cloud.

I grit my teeth, refusing to miss the feel of her body on mine.

Then I stand, holding my bound hands in front of me. As she marches alongside me, walking back to the cabin, I let my smile fade, like the stars winking away at dawn.

I'm certain that in a few hours I'll be on my way back to Manhattan.

12

———————

GABE

THE CABIN IS ONE OF THOSE SMALL, RUSTIC, WOODSY homes with wooden snow shoes hanging on the wall over the stone fireplace, a handmade quilt on the couch, and table lamps carved like bears and deer.

It's very up north woodsy. There's lots of golden knotty pine, the floors, the walls, the molding, it's all wood. And even though the cabin clearly has been vacant for at least a few months, it doesn't smell musty, instead it smells like wood shavings and fresh air.

You can tell that this is a family cabin—from the colorful balls of yarn in a basket by the couch, to the mystery paperback left on the side table, to the framed family pictures on the mantle—there is evidence of a happy life everywhere.

I work on unraveling the Christmas lights from my wrists as I take it all in.

The woman turns on all the lamps, bathing the room

in a golden glow, and then moves to the thermostat, cranking up the temperature. It's about fifty-five in here now, but even so, after the cold of the night the cabin feels like a tropical paradise.

I get the last of the lights loose and drop them to the wooden bench next to the door.

"What's your name?" I ask, and when I do the woman looks at me with wide eyes, as if she'd forgotten I was here.

"I thought you knew."

"Marley?" I ask, thinking of her obsession with Scrooge.

"No."

She gives a short huff of laughter and walks back to where I'm standing. She reaches down to pull off her fur-lined boots, dropping them beneath the bench.

"Not Marley," I say.

I stretch my hands, moving my fingers, letting the painful pricks of circulation come back.

"But I bet it's something Christmas related. All you nutters who love Christmas always have those kind of names. How about...Holly?"

She lifts an eyebrow. "Do you want me to tell you my name?"

"No, I'm going to guess it," I stare at her, take in her bright eyes, her curves, how she seems to fit perfectly in this homey rustic cabin. "Noelle."

She shakes her head.

"Mary?"

No.

"Ivy?"

Nope.

"Fruitcake?"

She snorts.

"Carol? Chris? Star? Rudolph?"

With each guess she shakes her head, and when I say Rudolph she actually lets out a strangled laugh.

"No. Wow. My parents wouldn't saddle me with the name Rudolph. They actually like me."

I look across the living room at the pictures on the mantle. There's a family photo from decades ago, a dad in a baggy sweater and wire-framed glasses, a mom in a denim dress, and a little girl hugging her younger brother while they all beam at the camera. They're all standing in front of a scraggly Christmas tree wrapped in paper chains.

"Hmm. I wonder what your mom and dad would think of your descent into crime." I frown at the picture of the happy family, then say in a mournful tone, "She was such a sweet little girl, kept to herself, nice to the neighbors, no one would've guessed what a devious heart lay beneath that Christmas façade."

She wags her finger at me. "Okay. Yes. *Some* might say this is wrong."

I give her a disbelieving look.

She grumbles, "But others might say that this is fate. Destiny. Christmas providence."

I shake my head. "No one would say that."

"Some might."

"No they wouldn't."

"Maybe two or three."

I shake my head. "No."

She sighs. "Fine. They wouldn't...or they might. My name is Natalie. Nice to meet you." She holds out her hand.

I let out a laugh. "Natalie. Which means Christmas. I forgot that one."

The cuckoo clock near the kitchen lets out a winding song, the tinkling notes of "Edelweiss" ringing out. Three dancing bears parade in a circle, trumpeting the twelve o'clock hour.

I smile sardonically at her and take her hand in mine, my grip firm. I ignore the chill of her fingers, the delicate softness of her skin, and the flood of warmth that flows over me at her touch.

Instead I hold her hand tightly and say, "Did it ever occur to you, Natalie, that I might be dangerous? You don't know me. You only met me today. I could have a criminal background. I could be a psychopath. I could have fantasies that involve wilderness cabins, a helpless woman, and a spoon."

"A spoon?" She frowns at me and tries to pull her hand back but I don't let her. "What the heck would you do with a spoon?"

I shrug, keeping ahold of her. "Some might say you could do a lot of things with a spoon."

She glares at me. "No they wouldn't. No one would say that."

I'm not sure what she's thinking, I just randomly

threw spoon out there, but if I can trust her expression, whatever spoon tricks she's thinking about, they're sick.

"Maybe two or three people would say that." I smile at her.

She takes a step back, I move with her.

"No," she says, scowling at me. We're in the living room now, near the couch with the hunter green bear-themed quilt.

She yanks her hand again, and finally I let her free. She's regarding me now with suspicious, distrustful eyes, glancing between me and the door.

"Where would you go?" I ask, "You're stuck here with me and my spoons."

I'm feeling better by the second. Natalie's cheeks are flushed, she's giving me a worried look, and I think, if she stays worried, I won't have to engage in any Christmas crap.

Or...on second thought. "You should probably call your parents. Nice people that they are. Have them bring out the car keys tonight."

Her eyes narrow on me. The ticking of the wall clock is loud as she says, "Oh really?"

I nod. "Yes. For your own safety."

She purses her berry red lips and then shakes her head. "Sorry. I got rid of the phones too. My family gets here on Boxing Day. Not before. We're stuck."

Apparently, she's decided that I'm not dangerous. Which, dang it, she's right. I'm not going to force, overpower, or...spoon.

We're stuck.

Together.

Unless she's lying about the phone and the keys. I'll search for them as soon as it's light. If they're anywhere, they'll be in the car. She'd have hidden them before opening the trunk.

At the thought of the cramped ride in the trunk, and her shoving me in the trunk while I was sleeping, my mood goes downhill.

"I'm going to bed," I tell her, walking toward the hallway off the kitchen.

"Wait," she calls, hurrying after me.

I wave my hand, ignoring her, moving down the dark hall.

There's a rug, a long braided runner over the wooden floor. More pictures on the walls and framed quilt squares.

There are only four doors, the first is a small bathroom, I poke my head in and see a bathtub, a sink perched on a wooden vanity that looks handmade, and a toilet.

The next three doors, standing opposite and kitty-corner to each other in the hall, are bedrooms.

Natalie hovers behind me, and I can feel her worry. "You aren't really dangerous, right?"

I wonder if she sees the irony in her asking the man she carted to an isolated cabin if he's dangerous.

I pause, my hand on the cold brass doorknob of one of the bedrooms, the one with plaid patterned curtains and a queen-sized bed. The shadows of the hallway stretch between us, but even in the dark I can suddenly see how tired she is, how she's swaying on her feet.

I shake my head. "I won't hurt you."

She nods then and steps toward me, the floors creaking under her feet. "Okay. Then I think...I don't trust that you won't try to leave and it's really not a good idea. You actually would freeze to death. So...I think...we should sleep in the same room."

I give an astonished scoff. "Really?"

"Just so if you try anything..."

"I could walk out of here right now and you couldn't stop me."

She considers this, then nods.

"True." Then her eyes light up. "Which means I didn't actually kidnap you, because you can leave anytime. I just *inconvenienced* you."

Wow, she's something else.

"Your penchant for moral ambiguity is appalling."

"Says the man who is evicting families for Christmas!"

I ignore that and step into the room, clicking on the nightstand light. The braided rug cushions my feet.

I shrug off my coat, drop it to the dresser, then loosen my tie. Natalie follows me in. The room is on the smaller side, the dresser and the bed take up most of the space.

I unclasp my watch and set it on the dresser, then ask, "What if I promised not to deliver the notices tomorrow?"

"Would you mean it?" she asks skeptically.

"Of course."

She snorts. "You are a *terrible* liar."

I nod. I always have been.

Behind me, the bed is piled with a thick comforter, a quilt, and flannel sheets. I yawn and roll my shoulders. "I'm going to get undressed. If you don't want to see this, you should go."

Her cheeks flame red as I unbutton my shirt, then shrug it off.

"You don't scare me," she says, pulling her atrocious Christmas bulb earrings out of her ears and setting them on the dresser with a forceful click.

I hide a smile as she tugs off her necklace and turns off the blinking LEDs.

I take off my undershirt, leaving my chest bare, then immediately wish I hadn't, because dang, it's still cold in here.

She purposely avoids looking at me, her chin in the air. I smile, then slowly move to unbutton my pants. At that, she practically sprints from the room.

I grin as I look around the empty bedroom. If I have to spend the night away from home then this isn't such a bad place. I've seen a lot worse.

The up north theme extends here, lots of plaid and black bears and wood furniture. It's comfortable, and thank goodness, not Christmassy.

I rub my hand along the back of my neck, trying to work out a kink from the trunk, and give a long sigh.

There's a noise at the door, a small creaking, but when I turn no one is there. But on the floor in the doorway there's a folded bath towel, a washcloth, a brand new toothbrush, and—I smile—a pair of men's sweatpants.

"What? No milk and cookies," I call, certain she can hear me.

Later, when I climb into bed—the flannel sheets cold and the room dark—I'm not surprised to find her slipping into bed next to me. The rustling of the sheets is loud as she slides in. Her scent wraps around me and her warmth seeps into the bed.

"Don't get any ideas," she whispers. "I'm just making sure you don't try anything stupid."

I smile, my arms behind my head, watching the starlight stream over the bed. In the city it's the building lights that bathe the bedroom, here it's starlight. It seems almost like a different world entirely.

"I never try stupid things. I'm the most deliberate person you'll ever meet," I say, my voice piercing the dark. I feel her stiffen, so I ask, "Are you sorry you brought me here yet?"

I wait, listening to the rumble of the old heater as it warms the cabin. It moans and whirs and sends dry warm air over us.

Finally, she shifts, looking over at me. Her profile is dark so I can't see her expression, I can only see the outline of her and her dark hair falling in tangled curls over her pillow. She's in a nightshirt and socks, and the blanket is tucked to her chin.

"No," she admits, "not yet."

Then she yawns, sinks down into her pillow and within seconds, her breathing evens out and she's asleep.

I was right. She was exhausted.

I get it. Since December arrived I haven't slept a single night through. An hour here, two hours there. I'm running on fumes, just trying to make it through the season. But there's something about the warmth of her, the softness of her breathing, the weight of her lying next to me, that feels like a benediction.

I close my eyes and for the first time in twenty-one nights, I fall asleep and I stay asleep.

13

DECEMBER 22, 8:31 A.M.

I WAKE SLOWLY, LIKE A SNOWFLAKE DRIFTING LAZILY FROM the sky, and find my cheek pressed against a warm, hard, naked male chest.

His dusting of hair on smooth skin, the beating of his heart, the rhythmic inhale and exhale gently pull me awake.

However, once I'm there, I fling back the covers and jump back like a scalded cat. My cheek burns, the hand that was resting on him tingles. I scramble off the bed, adjusting my flannel nightgown, yanking it down.

He blinks at me, then stretches and says with a yawn, "So it wasn't a nightmare. Too bad."

I scowl at him, my cheeks burning, my whole body

tingling and demanding that I jump back in bed and cuddle up with the warm, sleep-mussed man.

I scrunch my toes in the cozy socks my mom knitted for me last year and pull myself together. I have a mission, and that mission starts now.

"Nope. You're still here. And I know exactly what we're going to do today."

"Right. Sure."

He sits up in bed, displaying miles and miles of golden skin, taut muscles and a dusting of dark hair that leads down toward the blanket covering the rest of him.

I definitely didn't think through the sleeping situation, I was just concerned about him running off and freezing to death.

He swings out of the bed, stretching his arms over his head. I get an eyeful of his long, lean torso, the lines of his back and the thick muscles in his shoulders.

No wonder he was hard to drag, he's built like a lifelong athlete.

I'm five six and strong, but he wasn't joking when he said he could overpower me. It would be like a wolf tackling a puppy, not even a contest.

He's the exact opposite of Jason, the man I was supposed to be bringing home this Christmas. In every single way.

And then I realize something that's really depressing. I haven't thought about Jason at all. I thought he was proposing, I was going to say *yes*. Yet since he's broken up with me I haven't given him a thought.

Which means...that wasn't love. That was *like*. A

comfortable, pick-up-the-milk-on-the-way-home, spend-time-together-on-holidays-because-its-convenient like. I thought he was the reliable, always there, Christmas kind of love. He wasn't.

And apparently I'm not too broken up about that.

Gabe turns then and takes me in, standing there, ogling his backside. He shakes his head. "I hope your plan includes breakfast. I'm starving."

Of course it includes breakfast. Who does he think I am?

14

GABE

"I THINK YOU ARE A TERRIBLE PERSON," I SAY OVER THE upbeat Christmas carols blasting from the stereo.

The smell of maple sausage and pancakes fills the kitchen. I jiggle the coffee maker, trying to get it to brew faster. The thin stream of black liquid spills into the glass carafe.

"I know. That's okay. You can hate me. I'll be in good company with all things Christmas." Natalie waves her spatula at me, granting me permission to hate away.

Steam rises around her, the sound of sizzling sausage mixing with the beat of "Jingle Bells."

This cabin is stocked. I've seen preppers. Natalie's family must be full of preppers. They have a chest freezer full of meat and pre-made dinners. A pantry full of baking mixes, flours, grains, oils, dried eggs, dried milk. Everything you'd need to live off the grid for months.

I have to give it to her, this is the perfect place to bring a "guest" for a secluded getaway.

She even had a closet full of spare clothes. Hers and her brother's. He's a bit shorter than me, a bit wider, but it works. I'm in old jeans and a t-shirt that says Romeo H.S. Football.

Natalie is in a long red cashmere sweater and tight, hip-hugging jeans. She's swaying to the music, swinging the spatula like a conductor's baton. I fight a smile. If she weren't such a festive fanatic I might actually like her.

As it is, I can't wait to get away from her.

Back to the city and my life, which does not include Christmas.

"So today we're going to cut down a Christmas tree and decorate it."

I shake my head, "No we're not."

She stares at me, and I'm pretty certain she's surprised at my resistance.

The coffee has slowed to a drip, so I take down two mugs and pour the steaming black liquid, enjoying the rich smell. I shove one across the counter toward her and take a long drink of the hot liquid.

"Just like that?" she asks, frowning at me.

"Just like what?"

"No. Just like that?"

I take another sip. It's good coffee, then say, "Of course. What are you going to do? Make me?"

She pulls the pan off the stove and holds it high in the air. "Here's the deal. You come Christmas tree cutting with me and you get delicious sausage and pancakes. You don't...and you get...you get..."

"The lotion?" I ask straight-faced.

Apparently she's not a fan of horror, because she waves that away.

"No. Last year's fruitcake. It's in the cupboard, soaked in rum. And lemme tell you. It's fluorescent green and goopy brown. There are oozy bits. And when you take it out of the tin, it makes a squishy splooshy noise. Like it's exhaling."

I stare at her, appalled at her fruitcake description. Maybe she is a fan of horror. "This is a real thing? A breathing fruitcake?"

"Of course. You should see the one we're saving from 2012. Actually, maybe I'll give that one to you." She shakes the pan at me, the sausage smell drifting over. "You decide. Sausages and pancakes. Or respirating fruitcake."

"You are diabolical."

There's no way she knows that I can only cook two things: toast and microwave meals. And I didn't see any bread or microwaveables in the pantry. So...am I actually at her mercy?

I consider the pan of sausages, the maple scent drifting across the kitchen. It's a homey smell, sweet and savory, matching the warm wood cabinets and the butcher block counters. My stomach lets out a growl, reminding me of how hungry I am.

I haven't eaten since yesterday's lunch. A microwave

noodle bowl that I half-ate while going through emails and making calls.

I weigh the options. Go hungry. Go Christmas. Go hungry. Go Christmas.

"Fine. I'll kill a tree with you then decorate its carcass in lights and shiny balls." I take the plate from the counter and hold it out to her, "Serve it up. Even prisoners get two hots and a cot. Something you'll be learning very soon."

I smile at her. A little wickedly maybe.

She shakes her head, setting down the pan and sliding three sausage patties and a pancake on my plate.

"Thank you," I say, before grabbing the utensils and sitting on one of the stools at the counter.

"You're welcome." She sticks her nose in the air, then says, "Carcass, ha."

I eat then, and soon, I forget about the horrid Christmas music and the threat of tromping through the snow looking for a tree, and even about being trapped here for days, because, wow this good.

The sausage is maple and apple and crisp golden savory meat. It's local, handmade, it has to be. And the pancakes, she did something, I don't know what, but I think she sprinkled crack in them.

"What's in these?" I ask, shoving another bite into my mouth. There's maple syrup on the counter next to me, so I reach over and pour more on top.

"You like them?"

I make a noise, my mouth full.

She smiles at the unspoken compliment. "It's a

family recipe. Gingerbread pancakes. We keep the mix in the pantry. Ginger, cinnamon, cloves, dark brown sugar, vanilla. It's dried eggs and powdered buttermilk this time, because obviously I didn't go to the store, but it works, right?"

I stare at her. Works? I haven't eaten a homemade meal in years. She probably has no idea how much it works.

Suddenly, I feel like a stray dog, I've been fed a juicy bone and now I'm contemplating never leaving her side. Begging for handouts.

I frown, uncomfortable with the thought. "They're okay. I was hungry."

She shrugs and turns back to the stove.

I've finished. I don't want to ask for more, even though I definitely want more. But I don't have to worry, she slides two more pancakes on my plate and another sausage patty. Then she sits down next to me and digs in.

This time, I eat more slowly, watching her from the corner of my eyes.

She eats with unabashed enthusiasm, moaning happily and making little sounds of pleasure. Not that I blame her, these pancakes are ambrosia.

There's a dollop of maple syrup on her upper lip and I try not to look at it, or think about wiping it off—with my finger or my mouth.

I shake my head then push back from the counter, standing abruptly. I put my dishes in the sink and run the water over them.

"Ready?" I ask, suddenly enthused for freezing temperatures and hiking through the woods.

"You're excited?" she asks, surprised.

"No. Let's go."

She kept her end of the bargain, I'll keep mine. Then I'll go search the car and find my keys and my phone. Or hers.

15

———

NATALIE

THE WOODS ARE QUIET WITH THAT POST-SNOWFALL silence where the earth is blanketed in white and the sounds are muffled.

The morning sun lights blue, pink, and yellow crystals in the snow, a gorgeous prism of diamonds dancing over the winter landscape. For as far as you can see there's only glittering snow, dark green pine trees covered in snow, and the clear, winter blue sky.

I pull my coat tight around me, glad that we keep the cabin stocked with snow pants, boots, coats, extra gloves and hats, all those winter things.

My breath hangs in front of me, condensing in steamy puffs.

Gabe's taking long strides through the snow. It crunches and whooshes as he breaks through it. He's wearing Felix's boots. They're a little small but they work. I follow him, hopping into his footsteps, glad to let him break our trail through the deep snow.

I have the hand saw, the red-handled, carbon steel tool that my dad keeps with our gardening supplies. It has triple cut razor teeth and my dad makes sure it's sharp enough to cut up to a six-inch diameter trunk.

Ahead of us, a bright red cardinal perches on the snow-covered needles of a pine tree, but when it sees Gabe and me coming, it wheels into the sky, its fluttering wings echoing off the snow.

Gabe glances back at me, and when he sees me teetering in his footsteps, he shakes his head. "You should've pulled those snowshoes off the wall."

I frown, "Those are decoration. You can't use decorative snowshoes outside, it's against the rules."

He gives me a grin and lifts an eyebrow. "Since when do you follow rules?"

Okay. That's a good point.

But I say, "All the time. For instance, I always pay my taxes on time, I never double-park, if the cashier gives me too much change I always give it back, I follow the speed limit, I don't cut in line—"

"You're a paragon of virtue," he says. "I bet you were never on Santa's naughty list."

"Of course I wasn't."

"Well, you are now," he says with a smirk. "A lifetime of good behavior wiped out. Poof. Gone."

I narrow my eyes. "What about you?"

He strides forward, ignoring my question, kicking up snow as he heads deeper into the woods.

I hurry after him, sinking into his footsteps.

"How about this one?" He points at a four-foot-tall pine, scraggly and lopsided.

"Umm. No. I like them big, thick, not…" I trail off, that sounded unnecessarily suggestive.

He scoffs and starts deeper into the woods. Far off, the cardinal sings and another responds. I take in a breath, the cold pine and snow air, stinging my nose.

"This one then," Gabe says, pointing at an eastern white pine, with a grayish-brown trunk and soft, flexible, dark green needles blanketed in snow. A few pine cones hang down from the branches, not eaten yet by hungry forest animals.

I look over the tree, admiring the shape and the color.

"It's big. It's thick," Gabe says.

"Maybe too big," I say, thinking it would overwhelm the living room with its size.

"You are the Goldilocks of trees," Gabe says, rubbing his hands together then blowing into them. Even with gloves and hats, it's still freezing out.

He picks his way through the woods, and even though I should be keeping an eye out for a Christmas tree, instead I study him.

His cheeks are red from the cold, his dark hair tucked under a winter hat. He's in jeans, a Romeo football tee, boots, and his wool coat. There's something about the assured way he moves, the hardness of his jaw, and the confidence in his stride that makes me think he'd look good even if he were dressed in a paper bag.

I decide to distract myself from the tingling I get whenever I look at him. "So tell me, why do you hate Christmas?"

He adjusts his collar, pulling it higher, and ignores my question.

That's twice now. First he wouldn't say if he was on the naughty list, now he won't say why he hates Christmas.

"Is it because you got socks and underwear instead of that..." I try to think of what seven-year-old Gabe would've wanted for Christmas. "Dump truck you asked Santa for?"

He turns back to me, the sunlight sifting through the trees spreading between us, sending up prisms of light. "I see what you're doing."

He taps his head and gives me a meaningful look.

"What?" I ask innocently.

"You think there has to be some reason I hate Christmas. Some terrible event in my past. Some tragedy. You're holding out hope that I'm a nice guy burdened by a tragic past. Sorry, Marley, I'm just a Christmas-hater. What you see is what you get. This one." He points then, and I shake my head, confused. Until I see that he's pointing at a balsam fir.

It's a beautiful tree, six feet tall, with a full base angling up in a perfect triangular shape. The branches are full of thick, dark green needles and upright cones.

"Now that's a Christmas tree," I say, already imagining the tinsel and the lights.

Gabe grabs a branch and shakes the tree, sending up a blizzard of snow and a citrusy balsam scent.

I close my eyes as the momentary snowstorm flies around us, prickly and cold. Then, when I open them, the balsam is cleared of snow, green and full in all its glory.

"Yes," I say, "this one."

Then I kneel down in the snow, the cold pressing into my knees, and study the trunk. It's covered in a sticky sap, the fragrance like Christmas morning. "Okay, it's good. We'll cut through it in no time."

I stand and then look between the hand saw and Gabe. Usually, in my family, the person who picks the tree gets to cut it. But...

"What?" he asks.

I frown. "I was wondering whether I should hand you this saw."

He laughs. It's rich and warm and flows over me, tangling my insides and tying me up. "You don't think things through, do you?"

A smile lingers at the edge of his mouth, and if I didn't know better, I'd believe that he likes me.

"I admit, I'm impulsive. Act in haste, repent in leisure."

"When do we get to the repent bit?" he asks.

I smile at him then hold out the hand saw. "Cut it."

He takes it, his gloved hand brushing over mine. When he grips the saw, he says, "I wonder, did you think about the fact that when I don't arrive for work, my office staff will worry?"

I smile. "Of course I did, which is why I called in last night during the drive up and left a message on your assistant's voicemail. I said you were sick and would be out for a few days."

He stares at me, a disbelieving look on his face. "And you think she'll believe that?"

I nod. "Sure. I said, 'Good evening. Mr. Cavanaugh directed me to call and inform you he's out sick until December 26th as he's tired of Christmas. He expects to see you all back at work in the New Year. Merry Christmas!' and then I hung up. I think she'll pass the message on."

"You are a menace to mankind."

I nod. "I know."

"And my family? Don't you think they'll worry?"

I frown. I didn't think of that. He hasn't mentioned family. Although his business is named Cavanaugh and Sons, which means he surely has family. "Will they worry? Should I call them too?"

He clenches his jaw. "I thought you threw out the phones?"

Oh right. I did say that.

But the phones are hidden. And the keys...those are in a safe place too.

"Right. But...will they be worried?" I think about his mom, frantic because her son hasn't come home for dinner on Christmas Eve. His chair empty at the table, his presents wrapped under the tree.

"My kids will worry."

I stop, the sound of wind rushing through my ears. What's this? "Kids?"

He lifts an eyebrow. "What? I can't have kids? They can't worry when their dad doesn't come home?"

Oh my gosh...I'm a monster. He has kids, and they're at home, terrified because their dad never came home, and...

"Is there someone with them? Will someone take care of them? Did they...oh no, did they eat? Did they, are they, what..." I let out a little whimper, imagining his kids tucked in their beds, praying their dad comes home.

Gabe nods slowly. "Yeah. People have lives. You should have thought of that before you scrooged me. Now my kids are suffering. Terribly."

Wait. A. Second.

There's something about the look on his face, the way he's nodding, the tone of his voice. There's an itch inside that tells me...he's lying.

"You don't have kids."

"Sure I do. And since you feel bad we'll work together to get back to the city. We can't have them missing me for Christmas."

I cross my arms over my chest. "How many kids?"

He frowns, then, "Two."

"What are their names?"

"Their names?"

I nod. "Tell me their names."

He frowns and his eyes shift to the side, then he says, "Tom...and...Jerry."

I snort. Jeez. Unbelievable.

"You are the worst liar ever." I kick snow at him, and he dodges it. "You don't have kids."

He holds up his hands. "Fine. But I do have a dog."

My heart gives a little tug, and I almost fall for it, but then I see that nervous twitch of his lips and I know he's lying again. "You do not."

"How do you know?"

I point at his mouth. "Because you do this twitchy thing."

"A twitchy thing?"

I nod. "And you get this nervous look, and your voice goes scratchy, and look, Gabe, you're a terrible liar. Sorry."

He scoffs and then he narrows his eyes and says, "I do have houseplants that need to be watered. You can feel bad about that. You're sacrificing succulents."

I fight a smile. Gabe shakes his head at me and suddenly I wish that we'd met in the city, at the library, or in the park, and he'd asked me out for coffee and we...

The wind pinches my cheeks with its cold fingers and I shake out of the fantasy. This isn't about love, this is about Christmas.

"Get cutting." I gesture at the fir tree.

Gabe gives me a long, considering look, and I stand under his gaze, the cold air licking at me, the wind rattling the trees, and the cardinal singing.

I want to move, I want to shift, because his look does things to me, but I stand still.

And I wonder, does he have someone? He doesn't have a girlfriend, a dog, kids, but what about friends, parents, siblings? Or are houseplants the only company he has?

Finally, Gabe drops down to the snow and places the teeth of the saw against the trunk. Then the harsh, coughing sound of Gabe dragging the saw back and forth on the trunk fills the air.

The vibration of the sawing drops the rest of the snow from the branches. It whooshes to the ground, settling into the snow, and fills the air with crystals. The sharp citrusy sap scent grows stronger.

Gabe works at the trunk, his shoulders and arms moving rhythmically, cutting through the trunk quickly.

"Gabe," I say, and he pauses his sawing but doesn't turn my way, "Will someone be worried? Do you want me to somehow let them know?"

He turns to me then, his face in the shadow of the fir tree. "Let them know what? That I've been *inconvenienced* by a mistletoe maniac?"

"Well…" I shrug. "Maybe."

He shakes his head. "No need."

The sound of the saw fills the woods again, and now that the sun is rising higher, there are more bird calls and even, far off, the flash of a deer's tail as it runs through the trees.

With a shudder, the balsam tilts, wobbles, and then falls to the snow, a cloud whooshing around us.

Gabe stands then and says abruptly, "I have to use the…" He nods back toward the cabin, nearly indistinct through the trees.

His mouth twitches, his voice is scratchy.

I narrow my eyes. Is this a ruse? Is he going to...what? He doesn't have car keys. He doesn't have a phone. He can't actually go anywhere.

He gives me an innocent look, nodding back at the cabin and shifting on his feet. "I'll be back in a few to help."

Hmm.

He's not being honest, but really there isn't anywhere to go.

So I shrug. "No problem."

He smiles at me then, and my heart gives a little spin, like snow falling from the sky.

Then he's gone, jogging through the snow and the woods, the sky and snow bright against his retreating figure. Then it's just me, the tree, and silence.

"Alright, Christmas tree, let's do this." I heft the base of the trunk in one hand, the saw in the other, and then start slowly, awkwardly dragging the tree back toward the cabin.

I breathe heavily and a drop of sweat trails down my back, even though my nose is numb and my cheeks are burning from the cold.

The rustle-whisper of the needles scraping over the snow and the crunch of my boots in the snow is the only sound. That is, until the roar of a car engine cuts across the quiet.

I drop the tree and the saw. And then I run.

16

GABE

Clearly Natalie didn't think things through when she hid her car keys in a magnetic box under her bumper.

Amateur.

I smile as the car roars to life, the engine coughing and the freezing cold steering wheel vibrating under my hands.

The radio clicks on, blasting "Sleigh Bells," whinnying horses and jingling bells ringing loud. I jam my hand against the power button, bringing in blessed silence.

Then I back the car up, the snow crunching, the wheels spinning, trying to catch on the slippery surface. I rock it back and forth, maneuvering it around, and then I'm pointing away from the cabin, down the long, recently plowed drive. In the distance is the logging road.

I'll follow that until I come to a main road and then I'll find a gas station and make some calls.

I squint into the sun glaring off the bright icy snow. I push the gas, but the car fishtails and the wheel jerks to the side.

The car bounces off a high snow bank, the scraping noise loud.

The car is old, it coughs and moans as I ease it forward. The cold exhaust smell mixes with the fresh gingerbread still lingering. I frown at that and shake my head.

I won't be upset about leaving—stealing, no *borrowing*, Natalie's car. I refuse to acknowledge the twinge inside that grows larger as I drive.

I have a life.

A job to do.

And yes, eviction notices to deliver.

But something makes me look back. Just a quick look. Maybe I want a last glimpse of the cabin? Its rustic logs, the snow-covered roof and the glistening icicles hanging in front of the windows, the stone chimney, the snow piled high.

Or maybe I want to remember the woods, with their deep evergreens slumbering under blankets of snow?

Or maybe I think I'll see Natalie running after me, trying to stop me so she can bludgeon me with Christmas spirit?

Regardless, when I take a quick look back over my shoulder, I don't see her, I just see the cabin and the trees.

So that's it then. I'll head back to New York, notify the police...

I frown, suddenly weary, and turn back around to face the drive.

She's there.

Natalie's there.

She's ten feet in front of the car, standing in the middle of the snowy drive, waving her arms. Her eyes are wide, because, dang it, I imagine she expected me to stop. Not hit her.

But I wasn't looking.

I didn't know she was there.

I don't have time to stop. The road is too snowy, too icy, and as I slam on the brakes the car fishtails wildly. Snow kicks up, the car slides. Natalie stares at me, her expression stunned.

I yank the wheel hard, jerk it to the right.

The car slides. It's a great beast that I can't control, the wheel bucks under my hands, and I strain to keep it from yanking back toward Natalie.

It hits the snow bank. I slam forward, the seatbelt clamping down on my ribs.

The impact is loud. Snow flies over the hood, blinding me with white.

Then the car leaps over the snow, slams into the ditch, and jerks to a stop, crashing into a perfectly formed, perfectly green balsam fir.

My seatbelt catches me, yanking me back against the seat. And then the balsam snaps and collapses onto the hood. Snow and greenery rains down.

The car shakes, wheezes, and there's a pop as the front tire blows.

Finally, everything settles. I'm entombed in a coughing, moaning car. Not a speck of sky is visible under the fallen snow and needle branches of the downed fir tree.

But...Natalie.

I yank the seatbelt off. Shove open the door, pushing limbs aside and blinking through the falling snow.

"Natalie?"

There's a moan.

I jump out of the car, sinking nearly to my knees in the snow. There past the ditch, in the middle of the driveway, Natalie lies prone on the ice.

"Natalie," I call again, running through the snow. It breaks away, biting at my legs, the ice slipping down into my boots.

She doesn't respond. She's on her back, facing the sky, her arms and legs wide, like she's a kid making a snow angel. Her bright red sweater sticks out from her coat, and I can't tell, is that blood too?

Did I hit her?

Did I hurt her?

I slip on the drive, fall to my knees next to her.

Her cheeks are red, her eyes are closed. The ground is hard and cold, too cold. I don't know where the phones are. I don't know how to get help.

The car is buried under a ten-foot tree and a mountain of snow, its front tire popped. There isn't any way to get help.

What have I done?

I wanted to leave. I wanted to get back to the city, back to my life, but not in exchange for *her* life.

I throw off my gloves and reach forward, pulling at her snowflake scarf, loosening her collar. I press my fingers to her neck, trying to find her pulse. Her skin is warm still. Soft.

"Natalie," I say, leaning close, trying to feel her breath. "Natalie, talk to me."

My fingers press against her neck. Finally I find the solid thumping of her pulse. Thank goodness.

The warmth of her breathing tickles over my skin and I shift, looking down at her so our noses are almost touching. I let out a shuddering, grateful breath.

Then she opens her eyes.

And I realize for the first time that her eyes are green, almost the woodsy, festive green of a Christmas tree. I think, if you look into her eyes, you can't help but think of Christmas. Which usually would fill me with the desire to turn away, shut her out. But this time, I'm so grateful she's alright that I just stare into her Christmas-green eyes.

She stares back, her pupils wide, her eyelashes fluttering. Our breath tangles in white puffs between us.

"Are you alright?"

She reaches up and grips my shoulders. It's then that I realize I'm leaning over her, our lips are nearly touching, and I can already taste her—gingerbread pancakes, maple syrup, snow—and I can feel her—heat and abandon—and who am I kidding, I've wanted to kiss her since the moment I saw her.

All I have to do is move one breath closer, brush my lips over hers. "Natalie? Are you okay?"

She smiles at me then, her bright red lips curving. "Now who's on the naughty list?"

I stare at her, my mind foggy and clouded by thoughts of her mouth. "What?"

"You. Broke. My. Car." She jabs me in the chest to emphasize each word.

I blink. "You're worried about your car?"

"No. I'm worried about my insurance hike. Have you seen rates these days?" She shoves at my chest. "Where did you learn to drive? Jeez. You almost hit me!"

This can't be real. This moment can't possibly be real. My relief, my desire are all melting away turning to a smothering ball of anger.

"You jumped in front of a moving vehicle! Who does that?"

"You should've stopped!" She pokes at me again, driving her finger into my chest.

I lean closer and growl, "You shouldn't have kidnapped me."

"I didn't! I scrooged you! Because you are a cold-hearted bah humbugger and evictor of innocents!"

"Is that so?"

"Yes. That's so. Bah humbug!" she says, her cheeks flushed, her mouth pursed, her eyes flashing.

"Cold-hearted?" I ask.

"Cold-hearted," she repeats, her hand pressing into my chest, burning me.

So I do what I've wanted to for a good long while. I dig my hands into the snow around her head, block out the sun shining over her, and kiss her.

17

NATALIE

GABE'S LIPS ARE ICY HOT, LIKE SUN SHINING ON SNOW, bright and blinding.

As soon as his mouth closes over mine, all that cold from lying in the snow melts under his heat. He's blotted out the sun, all I can see is the dark shadow of his face, the sharp line of his jaw, his eyes closed as he makes a low noise against my mouth.

Then he's pulling at my bottom lip, tasting me and when I open to him, I can't keep my eyes open anymore. I close out the world, reach my hands to his shoulders, and hang on.

He lowers his chest over mine, cages me beneath him, presses me into the snow and settles between my legs. The snow gives way to our weight and we sink into the softness. His heat spreads over me, making my head spin.

He explores my mouth, sucking, tugging, licking. It's

as if he's making love with his mouth and every time he runs his tongue over my lips, I gasp and open wider for him.

His mouth is fiery heat banishing the cold, his breath a jagged, hopeful thing. I capture his kisses, taste him, sink into the flavor of maple syrup, ginger, and him. Heat not ice. Warmth not cold.

I brush my hand over his jaw, the stubble rubbing against my fingertips. His skin is cold, but his mouth is hot.

He turns toward my touch, bites my lip, crushes my mouth with gentleness.

I pull him closer, bury him on top of me, until we're touching everywhere, and even through our winter coats and sweaters and thick pants I can still feel him.

Fiery need bursts over me, so consuming that the only thing I want is to make love in the snow. Kissing him is like sipping warm mulled wine, naked in front of a roaring fire on a winter's night.

Decadent. Delicious. Necessary.

His teeth pull on my lip, his stubble rubs against my skin, his heat consumes me. The noises he makes, the low sounds in his throat, the sharp inhales, they're like gifts under the tree.

I want to gather it all to me and keep it forever.

But then he pauses. His lips remain on mine, but he's stopped moving, stopped making sound. Just stopped.

I wait, lie perfectly still beneath him. But as cold seeps over our lips, still pressed together, I open my eyes.

Gabe's staring down at me, his eyes as deep and

unreadable as a starless night. I stare back, my lips still pressed to his, tingling from his ministrations.

My blood pulses in my veins, a snowy blizzard fighting a conflagration.

I realize then that he's holding himself perfectly still. His hands are buried in the snow on either side of my head, his chest, his legs, his shoulders are tensed. Slowly, ever so slowly, he pulls his mouth from mine.

Cold air rushes in, robbing me of his warmth.

He clears his throat, his cheeks red, his mouth hard —even though I know it's not really—and says, "Where's my phone, Natalie?"

And...what?

After a kiss like that, he's thinking about leaving?

Oh wait. Of course he is. It's not like we're actually here on a Christmas getaway. It's not like we're lovers, or friends, or...anything.

He kissed me to, I don't know, prove he's not cold-hearted? But that didn't prove it, it only proved that he's a really good kisser. The best. Okay, the best ever.

I shake my head, suddenly feeling how very, very cold the snow beneath me is. I push at his chest. "Get off."

He frowns at me, giving me a look like he's disappointed in me, then moves to the side. Dang, it's cold out. His body heat was doing a lot to keep me warm.

"Natalie. My phone."

I shake my head and sit up, brushing the snow from my arms and legs. "No. I told you, we're here so you won't evict my friends on Christmas. And so that I can save your wizened heart from a lifetime of Christmas hate."

He makes a noise of disbelief, then asks, "Can you stand?"

I nod. "I wasn't hurt. Just stunned."

But then, when I try to stand, my ankle lets out a wincing, throbby pain.

"Ouch. Ow." I fall back down into the snow.

Gabe kneels next to me, touches my hand. "What is it?"

I nod toward my boot. "My ankle. I must have twisted it when I jumped out of the way."

His jaw clenches then and his mouth goes flat and hard. Then he leans forward, puts his arms under me, and lifts me as easily as if he's picking up a present.

"Hang on to me," he says, his voice rough.

I nod, swallowing down the rapid beating of my heart. As he strides past the car, covered in snow and branches, I bury my face into his warm neck and breathe him in.

He has a rhythmic, rolling stride. The snow crunches under his boots, the birds sing in the woods, and the wind blows cold and hard. I rest my cheek against his shoulder and stare up at the sky, light snowflakes beginning to fall around us.

At the cabin, he pushes open the door and strides quickly to the couch, setting me on it as if he's lived here forever and I'm the guest.

"Let me," he says, slowly untying my boot and then

gently slipping it from my foot. I wince at the stab of pain.

His fingers gently probe my ankle, running over my cold skin.

"Not broken," he says. There isn't any swelling, no bruising. It's just a little painful. I'll be right as rain in no time.

"Not broken," I agree.

He's kneeling on the floor next to the couch, cradling my ankle in his hands, his thumbs rubbing gently over my ankle bone and then up to my calf. I don't think he realizes he's doing it, because his eyes are distant and there's a frown on his face.

"It isn't safe," he finally says. "If something had happened, think of it, who would I have called? How would I have gotten help? It's time...you've had your fun...now let's go. I have a job. A life. You do too. Let's go back to the city. We can wipe out the last twenty-four hours. We can pretend this never happened. We never met. Alright?" Then more forcefully, "Okay?"

I shake my head. No.

"If we stay here for four more days." His voice is despairing as he takes in my refusal. "Natalie, someone is going to get hurt."

I keep shaking my head, so he gently lowers my ankle to the couch and stands, stepping back from me. The stone fireplace is behind him. The late morning light streams through the windows, and the warmth of the cabin is beginning to seep into me.

"Is my phone in the car?" He nods at the door. "I'll go get it now. Call a tow truck."

My chest clenches, my body freezes, as if I'm still outside, lying in the cold snow.

"You can't," I say.

"I can."

"You wouldn't." I give him a beseeching look.

"Of course I would." He shakes his head, turns to walk back out the door.

"Wait," I call, swinging my feet to the braided rug on the wood floor. I wince at the little sting of pain as I stand.

Gabe pauses, his hand on the doorknob. He's serious. He's going to find the phones. Make a call. Leave.

And although that's the logical thing, the reasonable thing, there's a voice inside me, soft but insistent, that says, *don't let him go, don't let him leave, not yet.*

"But what about Christmas?" I ask. "If you go, who will you spend Christmas with?"

He gives me a look that most people reserve for toddlers that just don't understand the way of the adult world, the one that says, you'll understand when you grow up.

"No one. I won't spend Christmas with anyone. I won't celebrate it. There's no reason. I'll be alone. Working probably. Which is how I like it."

I hold up my hand at that last sentence, because when he says that's how he likes it, his voice goes scratchy, and he looks to the side at the fireplace mantle where all our family pictures are, and I know he's lying. I know he is.

Miss Erma said that if I made Gabe experience Christmas it would fix everything. But he can't experience it if he leaves.

"Okay," I say, nodding. "I get it. I'm sorry."

He frowns at me, and I shrug, looking down at the rug.

"You're right. Someone could get hurt. We should go back to the city. Pretend this never happened. Pretend we never met."

I keep my eyes on the floor, my lips still tingling, my cheeks burning.

I hear Gabe let out a long breath, then the floors creak as he steps back toward the living room. Then he's in front of me, his smell enveloping me, his heat reaching out to me.

"You agree? We'll go back?" he asks, voice rough. Relieved.

I've never had someone so excited to forget about ever meeting me. Especially not after a kiss like that. Which makes me think it was a *lot* less enjoyable for him than it was for me.

I suppose, if I had any pride left, it'd be stung. But when I got dumped for a cat and then resorted to scrooging Gabe, I guess I threw out my pride.

So I nod. "Yeah. We'll go back. You're right. Let me just get your phone."

He grabs my hand then, squeezes it, and I look up, stunned to see a joyful smile on his face.

"I'm glad you came to your senses."

"Yeah." I take my hand from his, pull from his warm, strong grip. "I'll be back in a second."

Then before he can object, I limp out of the living room, down the darkened hall, to the second bedroom—my bedroom.

It's the same as ever, red plaid curtains, green rug, lumpy bed, Christmas lights twined around a bookcase chock-full of mystery paperbacks. I skip all that and head to the closet, push the coat hangers full of clothes to the side, and find the old shoebox decoupaged with magazine clippings.

I lift the lid and the smell of bubblegum lip gloss hits me.

I haven't opened this box since I was nineteen and I put away all the gag gifts my college friends gave me—virgin Natalie. They thought if they provided lots of toys, I'd be inspired. Well, whatever, I got there eventually and I didn't need this box.

But now I do.

Desperate times call for desperate measures.

18

GABE

I STAND AT THE WINDOW, MY HANDS CLASPED BEHIND MY back, staring out at the winter wonderland.

There's a frosted pattern on the window, a winter rose drawn on the glass by the cold winter night. I frown at the frost flower and keep my hands clasped together, resisting the urge to follow Natalie down the hall, lay her on the bed, and kiss her again.

I'd imagined that she'd taste like gingerbread, like candy canes—sugary sweet. She didn't. She tasted like addiction.

The second my mouth hit hers I needed more, and more, and I knew I would spend the rest of my life craving her, needing the feel of her.

The second I pulled away I felt the withdrawal. The only cure to the empty feeling is to kiss her again. Which isn't going to happen.

We're going back to the city. I'm going to forget about her.

I'm going to bury myself in mountains of work and make it through December. And contrary to the sudden burning desire to kiss her, I'm going to refrain. I'm going to forget about the Christmas nutter who dragged me to a cabin in the woods for a day and get on with my life.

Down the hall, Natalie limps back to the living room, her footsteps creaking on the wood floor. I don't turn to look. I don't want to see her expression.

There's a part of me that *almost* wishes she'd argued with me. The fact that she acquiesced so easily was a bit of a letdown. I've only known her for twenty-four hours, but already I expect her to fight for what she wants, give as good as she gets, come at me with passion and fire.

When she put her head down, stared at the floor, and humbly agreed that I was right? Let's just say it left me deflated.

Not that I want to celebrate Christmas or engage in her Christmas craze. But seeing her agreeing so readily? That wasn't her.

I narrow my eyes on her car, buried under snow and branches. There's an endless stretch of snowy wilderness.

Would Natalie give up so easily?

Would she?

Or is she planning something?

She's in the living room now, the soft sounds of her footsteps on the rug, her warm presence behind me. She steps close, lets out a shuddering breath.

I hold myself still, my hands clasped behind my back, determined not to turn around and kiss her.

"You have my phone?" I ask, my voice cold, strained.

Then, before I can turn around, or look at her, or do anything at all, cold metal locks around my wrist, biting my skin. The sound of metal clicking, locking is her response.

She's handcuffed me.

19

NATALIE

GABE TUGS, YANKS, POKES, PRODS AND PRIES THE handcuffs, but the fact remains, they're locked and we're not going anywhere.

His eyes are spitting fire, his jaw tight, his shoulders tense. He glares down at me, shaking his wrist.

My own arm shakes in response, the metal around my wrist chaffing my skin.

"You cuffed us together? With sparkly pink leopard print handcuffs?"

He seems more outraged about the sparkly leopard print than about the handcuffing.

I step close, only inches separating us, and lift my chin. "What do you expect? Marley's ghost had chains, why not me too?"

These handcuffs are solid, no getting out of them, at least not without the key. They're steel with a nifty automatic locking device and adjustable wrist sizes, which surprisingly works really well.

For a gag gift, these babies are solid.

"I know you want to leave," I say, trying to placate him, "but it's not happening. Not 'til after Christmas."

"You're something else," he growls, staring at my lips in a way that makes them tingle. "Come on. We're going."

He drags me through the living room, toward the front door.

"Where?" I ask, limping/hopping after him.

"To get the phones."

One slow trudge down the driveway later, I stand in the snow, my arm jerking as Gabe searches the car. I do my best not to look at the passenger seat. There's a hole in the side of the seat, covered by a vinyl patch.

I learned after my car was broken into that the hole is a really nice place to store valuables. The phones are cushioned by the foam and covered by the vinyl patch. Gabe doesn't even notice it.

After ten minutes of standing in the cold, my arm extended as he growls and curses, he admits defeat.

The sun is higher in the sky, the warmth falls over me, giving the cold day a cheery feeling. It's one of those perfect winter days where you build a snowman, head out on a cross-country skiing adventure, or...cut down a Christmas tree.

"Let's grab the tree on our way in." I nod toward the woods.

Gabe shakes his head, "You are the most single-minded person I've ever met. I don't know whether to be outraged or impressed."

"Impressed," I say, tugging him toward the woods.

"Outraged," he decides. Then he asks, his voice considering, "Are you seeing someone?"

He's studying my profile, but I keep my gaze straight ahead. It's more difficult to walk in the deep snow when Gabe's not breaking the trail. But now that I've handcuffed us, we have to walk side by side.

"I don't think you are," he muses, turning back to the white and green tree line. "If you were happy, satisfied in bed, in love, then you wouldn't obsess over Christmas and accost random strangers."

The back of my neck burns. "I'll have you know, I was seeing someone. I broke up with him yesterday."

Gabe stops. The handcuffs pull me up short. I turn back to him, the bright blue sky backlighting him.

"What?" I ask, more sharply than I intended.

"Yesterday? The same day you shoved me in your trunk?"

"It had nothing to do with it," I say.

He lifts an eyebrow, disbelieving. But he lets it go and says, "Let me guess. He didn't like Christmas either. Why didn't you bring him up here?"

I walk forward, picking through the snow, and Gabe follows.

"Oh, ohhh." He lets out a low delicious laugh, and it echoes off the snow and the ice. "*He* dumped you. What did it? Too much tinsel? Not enough kissing under the mistletoe? Salmonella eggnog?"

"It was his cat," I snap, stomping to the tree. We've made it to our balsam fir. I bend down and grab the trunk, the bark scraping my hand.

"What?"

I sigh and tug at the tree, pulling it over the snow. "He wanted to spend Christmas with his cat. Not me. Okay?"

For once, Gabe is speechless. I yank the tree, it's heavy, the boughs thick and full of shining needles. The citrusy balsam scent rises around us, and the sound of the branches scraping over the snow is a steady shoosh whoosh shoosh.

"I'm sorry, I thought you just said he dumped you for his cat."

"Mmm."

Gabe touches my arm and I pause, dropping the trunk to the snow.

"Please tell me that Cat is the name of another woman."

I snort. "No."

He grins, his eyes delighted. I shove at him and he laughs.

"Look who's talking," I say, "Why did your fiancée dump you?"

His chuckle slowly melts away, like icicles dripping in the sun.

"My fiancée?" He gives me a funny look.

"Delilah?"

"What? We were never...no."

"But...she gave you your ring back. She..."

"My *key* ring. To my apartment. We dated. Then she decided she didn't want..." He pauses, looks up at the wispy clouds puffing across the blue sky and considers his words, then he looks back at me and says, "An emotionally distant man incapable of living or loving."

I frown, thinking back to our kiss in the snow. "She's wrong."

He shrugs. "No. She was fairly accurate in her assessment."

I don't agree.

But he quirks an eyebrow and asks, "Isn't that Scrooge? You pegged me too."

I stare into his eyes and their fathomless depth lures me in. There's cold there, ice, but beyond that, I know there's fire too. I felt it.

"Come on." I nod at the tree. "Help me move this. It's heavy and I only have one hand."

He scoffs, "Whose fault is that?"

He says this with such gruff humor that I step close, stand on my tiptoes, and press my lips, tinged cold by the snow, against his.

20

———————

GABE

I can't stop thinking of her kiss.

We have the tree propped in its stand, pridefully placed in front of the living room window.

Our teamwork is a sight to behold. Probably because Natalie orders me around and I comply, all because I can't stop thinking about that three-second kiss.

Her mouth was soft, luscious, and welcoming. The sensation of kissing her is like an avalanche. With her lips on mine, I could only brace myself and pray I wasn't buried in the feel of her. Yet, I want to be buried. I'm standing on a mountain and I want the snow of her mouth to sweep over me.

"Isn't this fun?" she asks, handing the string of lights to me.

We loop them around the tree in tandem. Her cheeks are red, her hair is messy from her winter hat, and she has a humor-filled sparkle in her eyes.

The stereo is on, looping through the longest playlist of Christmas hits I've ever heard. They're not as grating as usual, probably because I'm distracted by the small, barely noticeable scar on Natalie's bottom lip. It's a thin white notch, disappearing into the pink of her lip.

"Fun? Decorating the tree with the lights you tied me up with? How could I not find this fun?"

Natalie grins at me. I wrap the lights around my side of the tree and then hand them back to her.

I've decided that being cuffed to someone is a bit like running a three-legged race. You both have to have the same goal and be headed in the same direction. If you're in opposition, you're going to fall down.

Natalie reaches for the lights, her fingers grazing mine as she does. Her touch is like the tiny Christmas lights, sparks that tingle and tease.

"What happened to your lip?" I ask, taking the lights from her and stringing them to the top of the tree. The needles poke my skin as I twist the lights through them.

Natalie reaches up and touches her mouth, a line between her eyebrows. "What do you mean?"

I tuck the last of the lights at the top of the tree then turn to her. We're standing close. We can't be any other way since we're locked together, but still I move closer. The tree branches brush my legs and let off a waft of evergreen.

"You have a scar," I say.

I drag my thumb across her bottom lip, feeling her silky soft heat. Her eyelids half close and her lips part. I graze my thumb over her, pulling her lip down, dipping my thumb into the wetness of her mouth. She drags her teeth over my thumb and I tug in a sharp breath of pine and her.

Slowly I pull my thumb along her lips, bring myself back from the brink.

"A scar," I repeat, my voice tight and low.

She blinks and shakes the haze from her eyes. "Our Christmas tree fell when I was a kid. One of the shattered bulbs caught me in the lip."

There's a warmth growing inside me, echoing the lyrics coming out of the speakers—*have yourself a merry little Christmas.*

"Only you," I say, shaking my head. "No wonder you cut down trees instead of using the fake ones. It's revenge."

She laughs, and the sound is like bells ringing. "Yes. It's my twenty-year-long revenge plot, executed with yearly diabolical precision. The trees must pay!"

I fight a smile. It's not too hard to imagine.

I glance at the pile of tinsel, the red and green bulbs, and the Christmas star laid out on the floor.

She pulled the decorations from a box in the garage, apologizing because they hadn't been used since the last Christmas they spent here, nearly twenty years ago. They were dusty, faded, and smelled of packing paper and cardboard.

"Tinsel next," she says, and when she steps to get it, I have to move with her.

She grabs the silver tinsel, all flash and sparkle, and I

help her wind it around the tree. The prick of the needles soothed by the softness of her hands.

"Why do you like Christmas so much?" I ask her, bending down to pick up one of the red bulbs.

She grabs a green one and hangs it from a bough in the middle of the tree. I place my red one near the top, where it catches the light from the lamp, sparking with a warm glow.

"How could I not?" she asks. "It's everything magical. It's everything wonderful and good and true, all wrapped in one day."

She smiles up at me, her face shining with what I've always considered the zealotry of the Christmas pusher. I've always thought that they're all the same, these Christmas fanatics, but now I'm curious. What makes her light up like that? And could *I* make her light up like that?

"Do you remember Christmas as a kid?" she asks, glancing at me from beneath her eyelashes.

A vision of a crooked Christmas tree, a red and green paper chain, gingerbread baking in the oven, and "Deck the Halls" sung with glee to the out-of-tune piano strikes me. I slam the door of my memory and lock it tight.

"We didn't celebrate." I avoid Natalie's gaze, bending down to pick up another green bulb, the glass cold on my hands, the hook poking my skin.

"Oh," she says, reaching down to take a red bulb. Her hair falls around her, the gingerbread scent of her drifting over me. "Well, I'll try to describe it for you then.

Every year when December arrived, my mom set out our advent calendar."

"Candy? Daily presents?" I ask dryly. From what I see, Christmas is all about selfishness and greed.

She nudges me with her shoulder, her body warm against mine. "No. Not at all. Each day had a tiny piece of paper rolled up and tied with a red ribbon. Felix, my brother, and I took turns unrolling them. Each day had a task that we had to do. Smile at a stranger. Give someone a compliment. Donate money to charity. Take cookies to a neighbor. Every day we did something to make another person's day brighter. My mom said that each day added up, and each little act grew and grew and grew, until on Christmas Day all that kindness was shining as bright as the Christmas star."

I stare at Natalie, at the pink in her cheeks and the way she's vibrating with the good of her memories. "Let me guess. This year one of the notes told you to handcuff a scrooge?"

She shakes her head, "No. Jeez. Who would do something crazy like that?"

I lift an eyebrow. "Who indeed."

She takes another bulb, and I bend with her, grabbing another to place on the tree. We're tucking them into the boughs, layering them in between the tinsel and the lights.

"Anyway," Natalie says, glancing at me, "while our daily advent went on, we also did all our Christmas traditions. There was tree cutting on December 1st—"

"The great day of revenge."

"Shush"—she waves her hand—"we'd pull out all our ornaments and tell the story behind each one. We have handmade wooden ornaments that my great-grandpa carved, ones my grandma knitted, and some that Felix and I made in school, clay handprints and glitter pinecones and...it's so wonderful pulling them out one at a time. It's like discovering a long-lost treasure. But you get to cherish it every year."

"Aren't you missing that, being here with me?" I ask, frowning at the happy look in her eyes.

She shrugs, the movement raising my arm too, since we're connected.

"It's okay. This is more important."

I shake my head. "It's not."

"It is," she says firmly. Then more quietly, "It is."

She picks up another bulb, and I do the same. We've almost placed all of them on the tree, spacing them evenly through the branches.

She stands on her tiptoes, trying to reach the highest branch.

"Let me." I gently take the ornament from her and loop the hook over the needles.

"Thanks." She smiles at me, then says, "After the tree is up, we always made cookies. Dozens and dozens. Sugar cookies with royal icing, gingerbread cookies, soft and chewy molasses cookies, peanut butter blossoms with that chocolate kiss, chocolate crinkles sprinkled with powdered sugar, pecan snowballs, you can't begin to imagine the sugary sweet smells that came out of our kitchen. We'd have a decorating party with all the neighbors and then we'd wrap up the cookies and share them."

"With who?"

"Everyone." She shrugs. "Teachers, our doctor, our mail carrier, the snowplow driver, my parents' coworkers, our friends, anyone, everyone."

"What if someone didn't want your cookies?"

She looks at me as if I've just sacrileged the great cookie god.

"That never happened."

"It happened with me," I argue.

She tilts her head. Frowns. Wrinkles her brow. Then she smiles. "We're making cookies after this."

I shake my head. "I don't want your cookies."

Her smile widens to a grin. "Yes you do."

I give her a forbidding look.

She shrugs. "Then after the cookies, we made Christmas snowmen and went ice skating and skiing. There was lots of hot cocoa all through December. And we wrote our lists for Santa and mailed them to his workshop in the North Pole."

"Doesn't exist."

"Says you."

"Says science."

She scoffs, then reaches down and grabs the last bulb. "The whole month is magic. But the best part is, all of it is full of family and friends. We're together for decorating, and sleigh rides, and Christmas dinners, and midnight services. We're together and it's so wonderful. I always loved dreaming up what present to get my brother and my parents. I'd think about it for weeks and weeks, and then I'd wrap it in homemade paper and put it under the tree. I always thought the best part of Christmas was watching them open the gifts I got them and seeing their faces light up."

She means it. She actually means it.

I'm startled. Stunned.

"What?" she asks, smiling at me.

"You make Christmas sound almost nice."

"It *is* nice."

She hangs the last bulb on the tree and gives a happy sigh. With her bright red sweater, berry red lips, she almost looks as festive as the tree. I clench my jaw and look away, staring at the cold frost pane of the window.

"What I like best about Christmas though," Natalie says quietly, "is how reliable it is."

Her tone is wistful and hesitant. I look back to her, but she's staring at a bulb on the tree, running her finger over the smooth glass surface.

"What do you mean?"

She leans down and picks up the star. It's burnished gold, with patterns carved in the metal, diamonds and swirls and tiny punch hole stars.

She rubs her hands over the metal, then hands it to me. I take the tree topper, the metal still cold from the garage. It's lighter than I thought it would be. I could easily twist it or crumple it in my hands. Instead I hold it gently.

"I only mean," she says, "that no matter what terrible things are happening in the world, no matter what troubles are in your life, no matter how hard things are, Christmas always comes. You can always count on Christmas. No matter what. It's silly, before I left for the city I told Miss Erma, you remember—"

"The soul mate lady."

I nod. "Right. My mom was worried about me leaving Romeo. She thought I'd never find my soul mate if I left. I told Miss Erma that and she said, *don't worry Natalie, Christmas always comes.* Which didn't really have anything to do with soul mates, but she gave me some advice then and I've kept it."

"What was her advice?" I ask, curious despite myself.

Natalie gives me a mischievous look. "She told me to find myself a reliable, Christmas-loving man who would love the presents I gave him."

I scoff. "She did not."

"She did!"

"Too bad. I guess I'm not your soul mate," I say dryly.

She stills. Gives me a stunned look. As if the very idea is too much to contemplate. But then she regroups and nods at the star in my hands.

"Will you do the honors? Put the star on the tree?"

I study her face, but the shock from my statement is gone.

"If I have to," I say.

"If you want that chicken and mashed potato lunch you do." She winks at me.

I shake my head. Cheeky, cheeky woman.

I put the star on the tree.

Natalie plugs in the lights, and even after all the

abuse I put them through, they blaze with gold-tinted white light, filling the room with a warm Christmas glow.

It's hard not to admire our work, except for the fact that Natalie's shifting on her feet, looking incredibly uncomfortable.

"What's wrong with you?" I frown at her as she crosses and uncrosses her legs and shifts some more.

She winces and then mumbles. "I mfft mfft ee."

I shake my head. "What did you say?"

Her cheeks flame bright red and then she says in an embarrassed voice, "I have to pee."

A slow smile spreads over my face. "You really, really don't think things through."

Now she'll have to unlock these cuffs. And then...home.

21

NATALIE

THE BATHROOM IS TINY WHEN THERE'S ONLY ONE PERSON, it's miniscule when there are two. Especially when one of them is a man over six feet tall with wide shoulders and a disapproving glower.

I stand backed against the vanity, my thighs pressed against the wooden counter.

Gabe's squeezed in next to me, and I realize that when he showered this morning, he would've had to duck since he's taller than the showerhead.

The bathroom should've been renovated years ago, but my family loves nostalgia. We voted to keep the faded pine tree wallpaper border, the woodshop vanity (Felix's eighth grade project), the pine cone balsam potpourri, and the hunter green bath accessories.

Gabe looks around the bathroom, the vanity light hitting his black hair, making it as glossy as midnight, then he looks back to me with a scowl.

"You want me to do what?" He shakes the folded Santa paws bedsheet like it's radioactive.

I cross my legs and give him a pleading, wide-eyed expression. "Pleeeease."

I'm going to burst. I'm literally about to lose it. All that coffee hit at once and now...oh my gosh.

"Just uncuff us," he says in a measured, patient tone. "Then you can have all the privacy you need."

"Ha. And while I'm in here, you'll be tearing this place apart looking for your phone."

He lifts his eyebrows but doesn't deny it.

"Please. Just hold up the sheet so you can't see me. And don't peek."

He gives me that *are you out of your mind* look that usually makes me smile. "Why would I peek?"

"I don't know." I cross my legs, then recross them, and then do a little jump-up-and-down dance. "Please. Please."

He sighs. "Fine."

Thank goodness.

He unfurls the sheet, displaying it in all its Christmas-pup-in-a-Santa-hat splendor. Then he holds it high above his head so that we're separated by a seven-foot-long fabric barrier.

Sort of.

I mean, our hands are still cuffed together, so the sheet has to fold around our arms. But it's a start.

"Okay, I'm just going to..." I scoot over to the toilet and then try to undo my jean's button with one hand.

My gosh, it's impossible. Who makes these buttons?

What's wrong with them? Didn't the button makers ever think that someone may need to unbutton their pants with one hand?

"What's wrong?" Gabe asks from behind the sheet.

I keep fumbling at the button. My word, it's like a chastity belt. It knows there's a man in here with me and it's trying to prevent me from dropping my pants.

"I can't get my button undone with only one hand," I say, squeezing and praying.

"Really?"

"Really. It's hard. Have you ever tried it?"

"On a woman's buttons? Or my own?" he asks, like he needs that information to give me an accurate answer.

"Come closer," I say, "so I can use my other hand."

He sighs and steps closer, the sheet drapes over my arm and then waffles over my face. I bat it aside. Then I tug my other hand close. His is there now too. His arm, his hand, reaching from under the Christmas puppy sheet.

Oh gosh, it's like the gynecologist but more festive. Hand. Sheet. Urine collection.

"Don't touch anything," I tell him, gripping my button with both hands and pulling it free.

"Relax. I'm not going to touch your button."

My zipper's next. His hand jerks as I yank it down, the zzzzfft of the zipper loud. The cuffs rattle as his hand yanks down with mine.

The sheet vibrates and jolts. He's moving up and down with me, his arm jerking. Now I just have to shove my jeans down. They're skin tight, so this is going to require two hands.

But now that my button is free, my bladder has decided it's go time.

"I'm pulling my pants down. Just move with me. Squat or something." I tug on my pants.

"Squat?" He doesn't move. The cuffs keep me from pulling my pants any further.

"Yes! Squat! Squat! So I can take my pants down."

He bends down, keeping the sheet between us.

I yank at my pants, tugging them over my hips. As I shove them down to my knees, yanking my panties with them, Gabe drops the sheet.

He curses.

It lands on my head.

I swing my arm, the sheet blocking out the bathroom light. Gabe's hand brushes over my bare hip and I jerk like I've been burned. I fall to the side and land hard on the toilet.

Gabe grabs the sheet, holds it high again. "Sorry. Sorry."

I close my eyes, mortified.

My arm stretches between the two of us, Gabe's taken a step back to give himself and the sheet of modesty room to hang.

It waves and ripples like a flag. The little golden dogs in Santa hats stare at me with big black puppy eyes. Behind the sheet I can hear Gabe breathing, moving, waiting.

I...can't go.

"You okay?" he asks.

"I need you to sing."

"Excuse me?"

"I need you to sing at the top of your lungs...sing me 'Jingle Bells.'"

There's a stunned silence. Then, "Are you out of your mind?"

I squeeze my eyes shut tight. "I can't go if you can hear me. I need you to sing. Please. I'll owe you."

I can feel his intent interest through the sheet. "You'll owe me?"

"Yes. I'll owe you."

"What will you do for me?"

Basically, right about now I'll do anything. "Anything. Within reason. No phones. No cars. Christmas fun isn't negotiable. But anything else."

That does it.

"You owe me then," he says.

Then he starts to sing in a loud out-of-tune voice that echoes over the bathroom tiles, "So this is Christmas and what have you done? Kidnapped a man, and shoved him in a trunk. So this is Christmas, I hope you have fun, because you're going to prison when all this is done."

As he continues his terrible rendition, I smile in sweet, blessed relief.

But the relief fades when I realize I'll have to go pee again sometime soon (and so will he) and then I'll have to sleep (and so will he) and shower (and so will he) and change into pajamas (yes, and so will he), and...then he'll call in his debt.

Gabe's right. I really don't think things through.

THE BUTTERY GINGER SMELL OF CHRISTMAS COOKIES warms the kitchen.

The sugary scent curls through the room, like white icing swirled over a gingerbread house roof. The taste of butter, brown sugar, cinnamon and ginger lingers, even though I haven't even had a nibble of the cookies yet.

There are a dozen gingerbread men cooling on a wire rack, waiting to be decorated. They are golden brown, plump, and perfectly formed.

Natalie is a master of Christmas cookies.

I'm stunned that we were able to work in tandem so seamlessly. I pulled the mixing bowls and hand mixer from the high cupboards. She found the ingredients in the pantry and the freezer. She scooped, I leveled off. She poured, I mixed.

When it came time to roll, we both took one end of the rolling pin and moved together so that the dough was an even quarter inch. Then she held my hand while I pressed the cookie cutter into the gingerbread dough. Gently, she'd said, don't tear the dough.

The whir of the hand mixer fills the room as Natalie finishes mixing the icing. The bowl rattles and spins so I reach out and hold it in place. Natalie grins at me.

"Thanks."

I nod, holding the bowl as soft white peaks form in the sugary icing. As the bowl vibrates against my hand, and the gingerbread smell surrounds me, I try to imagine what life would be like if this moment were actually mine. If Natalie and I were together, if I loved Christmas as much as the man she's hoping to end up with, if this were actually my world.

She was right when she said earlier that Christmas always comes. It's reliable. For people like Natalie, that's reassuring.

But for people like me? Christmas is the hot poker that reopens wounds barely healed over. It's a month of sleepless nights and trying to avoid memories triggered by crooked trees, shining lights, gingerbread and red paper-wrapped presents.

Natalie whirs the mixer through the bowl, spinning the sugar into glistening icing. She smiles up at me, her eyes warm.

If this were my life, then I'd kiss her. Right here, right now.

In years past, the Christmas trees, the lights, the smells, they all sent a wave of grief crashing over me. That pain would threaten to consume me. Then later, the pain receded, leaving only its bitter aftertaste. It left me hating Christmas and all its false cheer.

The fact that this is the first time in years that I haven't cringed at the smell of gingerbread or spurned the sight of a Christmas tree is probably, in Natalie's words, a Christmas miracle.

She turns off the blender, the quiet a welcome relief. I dip my finger into the bowl, swipe a bit of the icing and stick my finger in my mouth. It's pure creamy sugar.

Natalie swats at me. "Hey. No cheating."

I lick my lips, the sugar almost too sweet. "I'm quality control."

"Hmmph."

I turn my head and smile. She pulls over a freezer bag. "Hold this while I fill it please."

I hold the plastic bag open, and she spoons in great heaps of frosting. When it's full, she takes a pair of shears and snips the end of the bag.

"Okay. Decorating time. Icing"—she holds up the bag—"sprinkles and colored sugar"—she points to the tray of red, green, and rainbow sprinkles and the red, green, and silver glittering sugars. There are even sugar snowflakes, edible silver balls, and sugar poinsettias. "You can decorate any way you like."

"And then what?" I ask as she pulls the tray of cooled gingerbread men toward us.

"Then we eat them. We gorge ourselves on them." She tilts her head. "In front of the fire. With hot cocoa."

While she's talking, she squeezes the bag and a thin line of icing spreads onto the gingerbread man. She draws pants, sleeves, buttons down his front, eyes and a smile. "There. See? Do your worst."

I raise an eyebrow and take the bag. The frosting is soft and pliant in the bag. I squeeze gently, working quickly to draw the pattern I want. Stripe. Stripe. Stripe. Frown. Slit eyes. Number on chest.

"Is that—"

"Inmate gingerbread man."

She scoffs and grabs the icing bag from me. I shrug and grab the sprinkles and douse him in gory red sugar.

"Do you really want me punished?" she asks.

She doesn't look at me, instead she concentrates on forming perfect buttons on her cookie, pressing silver sugar beads into the icing.

I take a moment to look at her profile, her freckles, her button nose, the way her mouth can flash from mischievous grin to sweet smile in an instant.

"Yes."

She looks up quickly, her eyes wide. "You do?"

"Yes." A thousand times yes. A lifetime of yes. An image flashes in my mind, so real I can almost taste it. Natalie is on the counter, her legs spread, her head thrown back, and I'm inside her, my mouth on her breast, tasting her.

She must see something in my expression because her cheeks flush red and she reaches up to touch her lips.

I watch her fingers hover over her red lips, watch her teeth graze her bottom lip.

Slowly I reach over to the bowl and swipe my finger

through the remaining icing. She watches me, her pupils dilating.

"Do you..." I hold up the cool white icing covering my pointer.

She watches me, leans closer.

I hold my finger to her lips, let her open to me. She takes my finger, wraps her warm, wet mouth around me and sucks the white frosting from the tip. Her teeth nibble at me, her tongue swirls around me, and then she takes a long pull, sucking the frosting free.

Her eyelids lower, her warm mouth consumes me, and every suck and nibble tugs on me.

I press my finger deeper into her mouth and she makes a noise low in her throat and sucks me. With each tug of her mouth the rest of me responds, pulling closer to her.

I want her. I want her so much.

I want to lift her onto the counter, slip inside her and forget about Christmas. Forget it all.

Which is what makes me pull back, slowly take my finger from her mouth. She bites it gently as I tug free.

I clench my hand. Drop it to my side. It takes all my willpower not to lift her onto the counter and paint her in frosting and sprinkles and then devour her. That is not the punishment she's asking about.

Natalie clears her throat, her blush fading. "Well... the icing is good."

"It is," I agree, a hungry ache inside.

"I imagine you'd love Christmas if you got to have that every year."

I nod. "Maybe I would."

She tilts her chin, stares into my eyes, and even if I'd never seen an invitation to kiss, I'd know that right now she's offering her mouth up as a gift.

I bend down, my lips an inch from hers, when I hear it. The sound of a car engine echoing off the trees and tires crunching over snow.

Someone is here.

NATALIE

I RUSH TO THE KITCHEN WINDOW, MY HEART POUNDING madly, not from the approaching car but from the desire to sweep the gingerbread off the kitchen counter and make wild, messy love.

Gabe stands next to me, his presence as hot as a yule log roiling with orange and blue flame. The back of my hand brushes against his, the metal cuffs clanking together.

"Who is it?" he asks, his voice unreadable.

I peer out the kitchen window at the silver SUV slowly pulling around the wreckage of my car. They'll be inside in minutes. I glance down at my outfit, at Gabe, wearing Felix's jeans and shirt.

My mind races, my insides turn to jelly, and slowly Gabe gives me a satisfied smile.

"Time to pay the piper?" he asks, nodding at the SUV.

I turn, pace the kitchen, dragging Gabe behind me. The gingerbread smell, the toasty warmth, the sweet cabin in the wilderness, my wish that Gabe will see the light and not evict my neighbors for Christmas, it all disappears like icicles melting in the sun.

Because my family is here—four days early.

The SUV pulls to a stop in front of the cabin, the engine cuts, and then my dad, my mom, my brother, and for crying out loud, my grandma pile out of the car.

"This isn't happening," I say.

Gabe smiles at the noise of car doors slamming. "It looks like I am going back to the city today."

"They'll think you're Jason," I say, watching my mom point at my poor little yellow car squashed by the giant evergreen. "He was supposed to come to Romeo with me."

My mom has to be wondering what happened. I only sent her a text, telling her something had come up and I wouldn't see them until Boxing Day.

"Jason. The cat lover?" Gabe's lip curls, like he can't believe I even suggested that my family will think he's him.

I nod. "Yes. Perfect. You'll be Jason."

My family expects to meet him. My mom will be overjoyed.

Gabe shakes his head. "I'm not Jason."

"You could be."

"I could not."

"Some people might think you look like a—"

"No people would think—"

"Two or three might—"

"No."

We glare at each other, the winter light from the kitchen shining over us. I give him a smile but he only scowls and shakes his head.

"No go. As soon as your family comes in, I'm letting them know what a diabolical child they raised. And then I'm getting out of these cuffs"—he shakes them, making our wrists clank together—"and going back to the city."

I lean forward, so close our noses almost touch, and give him a hard glare. "To deliver those eviction notices?"

His eyes flicker with surprise at my question, then resolve. "Why else?"

I'm disappointed. I can't hide it. I know he's only been here since last night, but I thought...I'd begun to believe he wasn't such a scrooge.

I lean back. "Fine. You're not Jason."

He gives a jerk of his head. "Darn straight I'm not."

Then he reaches up, grasps my chin in his hands, tilts my head up and presses a punishing kiss to my lips. It's a kiss full of icing, sugar, and frustration. Tongue, hands, lips, breath. He kisses me like it's the first time he's ever kissed a woman and also his last.

Then the door bangs open and we jerk apart.

THE BACK DOOR BLOWS OPEN, SWEEPING FRIGID COLD AND a white bluster of swirling snow into the kitchen.

There's a man in the doorway, average height, gray hair, the serious, studious look of a college professor. I recognize him immediately from the photo in the living room. He still wears the same wire-framed glasses he sported two decades ago.

It's Natalie's father.

I roll my shoulders, push the kiss to the back of my mind. It's time to finish this festive farce. Natalie's gaping at me like I've sprouted another head, but I ignore the messages she's trying to send like Morse code from her eyes. Blink, blink, dot, dot, dash.

I think that means, please don't tell my parents I'm a mistletoe maniac.

I have to admit, I was tempted to smooth over

everything, leave with as little hubbub as possible. But then she had to go and throw the evictions into the mix.

I know she thinks I'm a cold-blooded, hard-hearted scrooge. I know this. I just forgot.

So I'm leaving and I just kissed her goodbye.

Natalie's father stomps into the kitchen, snow falling from his boots onto the mat.

"Natalie," he calls, his voice booming across the cabin.

Her mother, same brown curly hair as in the picture, same long denim-style dress under her red wool coat, pushes past her husband. The entry is tight and she hurriedly unwinds the green knitted scarf from her neck.

"Natalie?" she calls. "What happened to your car? Are you okay? Natalie?" She turns to her husband. "Where is she? Why didn't she call? What happened?"

Natalie pulls me with her, we step around the cabinets, and she gives a small wave. "Hi Mom. Hi Dad. Merry Christmas."

Her mom's hands fall from her scarf and flutter in front of her like she's sweeping aside snowflakes. Her dad's eyebrows lift high over the rim of his glasses, and then he takes me in, making a quick, analytical calculation.

I'd bet good money that Natalie's dad is the logical, even-keeled one of the family.

"Why...you brought Jason. How lovely," her mom says, rushing forward.

She envelops me in a warm hug, the snow from her coat falling over us, the scent of Christmas cookies and coffee strong. Her cheeks are round and pink and when she smiles up at me I can only think that she's the reason Natalie loves Christmas. Her mom is a young Mrs. Claus.

Good manners would dictate that I give her an awkward pat or hug her back, but since I'm currently handcuffed to her daughter, it's not exactly possible.

She doesn't notice. She's too excited. She pulls Natalie in for a hug, kissing her cheek.

"You look wonderful! I was worried you weren't eating well in the city with how busy you've been, but I shouldn't have worried. When I called Mrs. Givenchy she told me you were fine, but still...I can only send so many cookie care packages and restaurant gift cards."

"Hi Mom," Natalie says, her voice muffled by her mom's wool coat, "I missed you too."

"Yes. And luckily you have Jason to take care of you." She pulls back from Natalie and smiles at me, as if I'm a present under the tree. "I'm so glad to meet you."

She holds out her hand to shake mine. Out of the corner of my eye I see Natalie's cheeks flame red. Yes. She should be embarrassed.

My right hand is the one cuffed to hers. I lift mine, the sparkly glitter pink leopard print cuffs clank like the doors of a prison cell.

"Nice to meet you. My name's Gabe Cavanaugh."

Natalie's mom stares at my hand, her smile faltering, her eyebrows coming together in confusion. Natalie's dad steps forward, stares at the handcuffs and then glowers at me.

"Gabe Cavanaugh, is it?" he asks in a well-modulated

tone. It sounds like the voice a lecturer would use when he's about to tear a student a new one.

I shift on my feet, realizing with some discomfort that he thinks they interrupted Natalie and me playing naughty and nice with the cuffs.

It's that moment that the rest of the family bangs into the kitchen.

Felix, Natalie's brother, is carrying two large shopping bags stacked with wrapped gifts. He has dark curly hair, just like Natalie, but instead of a ready smile like his sister, he seems to have mastered the stern, studious look of his father. He's in his mid-twenties, and just like I thought from his clothing, he's a tad shorter than me, and a bit wider, with the physique of a football player.

Behind him, an older woman with white hair, owlish eyes, and a lime green fur coat stomps into the kitchen. She's holding a leopard print suitcase in her hands. Now I know where Natalie got her taste for leopard print from. Grandma, I presume.

Felix drops the sacks of Christmas presents to the kitchen floor, swaggers to the counter and grabs the gingerbread cookie Natalie decorated. He takes a bite while frowning at Natalie and me.

"Natalie. Why are you and Jason wearing handcuffs?" His eyebrows rise, and he takes another bite of the cookie. "These are good, by the way."

"He's not Jason," Natalie's dad says, giving me a stern look, like I've participated in some scheme to bamboozle all of them out of their Christmas gifts.

"His name is Gabe," Natalie says, her voice only shakes a little, and if I didn't know better I'd say she was thrilled to introduce me to her family. "I brought him to the cabin to celebrate Christmas. We didn't expect you all so early."

The last is said with a bit of censure.

"We voted," the grandma says. She takes off her coat to reveal a baggy sweater covered in gold sequin Christmas trees. "Since you texted that you weren't coming up, we decided to come to the cabin early, spend a nice old-fashioned Christmas in the woods. Like the good old days. When I was a kid we took sleigh rides, made maple sugar candy in the snow, and sewed rag dolls for presents."

"Mother please," Natalie's mom says, "that was Laura Ingalls Wilder. When you were a kid you watched Christmas movies on TV and went shopping for presents in the city."

"Well, if you want to be *accurate*," Natalie's grandma says.

Felix shrugs and shoves the rest of the cookie in his mouth. "Anyway, handcuffs Natalie? Ghosting mom's texts? Really?"

Natalie ignores her brother. "Everyone, this is Gabe. Gabe this is my mom Roberta, my dad Jerry, my brother Felix, and my grandma Agnes."

As Natalie introduces her family, her mom gives me a shining smile, her dad nods cordially, her brother gives me a skeptical look, and her grandma studies me like she's trying to decide whether or not I'm past my sell-by-date.

"I thought you were getting engaged to that web guy?" Grandma Agnes says, frowning at Natalie. "In my day we didn't jump from man to man."

"Jeez, Grandma," Felix mutters, grabbing my inmate cookie.

"Mom," Roberta says, "you had four husbands."

"And all of them were a delight," she says. "Your father included."

Okay. Now's the time to end this, while Natalie's family is still in their coats and their SUV is still warm and ready to drive out of here.

I hold up my hand and everyone looks at me. "While it's nice to meet you all. I need you to listen to me. Your daughter and I are not together."

"Oh jeez, I knew it," Grandma Agnes mutters. "She takes after me. Sees an attractive man and just can't help herself."

"Explain yourself," Jerry says, frowning at the handcuffs.

"Gladly," I say. "I only met your daughter yesterday. Last night she tied me up with Christmas lights, shoved me in her trunk, and then drove here to force me to participate in Christmas fun. She handcuffed us together to prevent me from leaving."

I stare at her family, letting them see the seriousness of the accusation by the gravity in my gaze.

Felix has the gingerbread inmate halfway to his mouth, a stunned look on his face.

Roberta shakes her head and stutters, "But...but..." while her hands flutter in front of her.

Jerry gives Natalie a hard, searching look.

Grandma Agnes just looks impressed.

Then I look at Natalie as does everyone else.

She's giving them the cheekiest, perkiest, biggest smile I've ever seen. Her eyebrows high and her cheeks red. She looks like a mischievous elf about to make trouble.

And then, the craziest thing happens.

Roberta starts to laugh. Then Jerry does too. Felix scoffs, shakes his head and bites the arm off the gingerbread man.

Grandma Agnes crows with laughter. "That's a good one. I love jokes, what a delight."

Roberta finishes pulling off her scarf and starts to take off her coat.

They don't believe me. They think I'm joking.

"Let's go unload the rest of the car," Jerry says to Felix, nodding to the door.

"Wait," I say, "I'm not joking. I'm here against my will. I need you to convince your daughter to unlock these handcuffs so I can go home. I'd like to borrow your car to drive to the nearest town. This isn't a laughing matter. I'm serious."

Jerry hesitates. Felix frowns at me.

"Natalie?" Roberta asks, looking between Natalie and me.

Natalie smiles up at me, then beams at her family. "Gabe's a method actor."

What?

"I am not—"

"You know the type. The one's who immerse themselves in a role. He's auditioning for an Off-Broadway kidnapping show. He can't break character, he's very dedicated. You know these actors. They take their craft seriously. Just go with it."

"Ohhh. I've heard of those," Roberta says nodding.

"Wow. An actor." Grandma Agnes lets out a delighted sigh, her owlish eyes widening.

"No. This is absurd." I shake my head, realizing that her family is buying this nonsense.

They *believe* her.

"He can't admit he's an actor," Natalie whispers. "That would break character."

"Well what are we supposed to do?" Roberta asks Natalie, actually concerned for my *acting*.

"You're supposed to uncuff me and drive me to the nearest town," I say, shaking the handcuffs at her family.

But Natalie says, "You can help him get the role by just going with it. He's method acting, so right now, he's been kidnapped for Christmas and he doesn't want to celebrate."

"What kind of roles have you had?" Jerry asks, studying me anew, assessing my chops as an artist.

"Dad, don't take him out of character," Felix says, shaking his head.

"I'm not an actor," I say, gritting my teeth. "I'm in real estate."

"In the play," Natalie says, "he evicts people for fun. On Christmas."

"Ohhh, a villain," Grandma Agnes says. "I always root for the villain."

I shake my head. Unbelievable. I step forward, level my gaze on Natalie's family. Give them a look that would scorch the earth and then salt it with my wrath.

"Listen to me and listen carefully," I say, clenching my hands. "My name is Gabe Cavanaugh. I am a real estate professional from New York. I was kidnapped by your daughter. I do not want to be here. I loathe Christmas. Everything about Christmas. If you don't want to be implicated in this crime, you need to uncuff me now and drive me to the nearest town. I am not an actor. I am not here to spend Christmas with you. You need to let me go. Right. Now."

The kitchen is silent. It's a stunned silence.

Good.

I've gotten through to them.

I take a deep breath, unclench my hands, and that breaks the spell.

Roberta claps her hands, Grandma Agnes cheers, and even Jerry slaps me on the arm.

"Great acting, you're amazing!" Jerry says. "Incredible."

"That was excellent," Roberta gives me a wide smile. "You're very talented."

"Not bad," Felix shrugs, "for Off-Broadway."

I'm speechless, my head jangling with their claps and congratulations.

"He is good, isn't he?" Natalie says, smiling at her family.

My word.

They're all insane. They're all just as deluded as she is.

"This is going to be a wonderful Christmas. I love actors," Grandma Agnes says as she struts into the kitchen, aiming for the coffee maker.

"Come on then, Felix," Jerry says. "Let's get everything out of the car."

"But...no. I'm not acting," I say desperately, "I'm not an actor. I'm serious."

Roberta pats me on the arm, a motherly expression on her face. "We know dear. We won't mention it. Don't want you to break character. We'll play along as much as you like."

"No." I shake my head.

"See, Gabe, I told you they'd understand," Natalie says.

She gives me a cheeky smile. I stare at her and I have the strongest urge to take her in my arms and...well, I block out what'll happen next.

"An actor," Grandma Agnes says. "I always liked actors. You look a bit like Cary Grant. Now *he* was an actor."

Felix and Jerry are heading out the door, the cold wind blowing into the kitchen, and as they leave, Felix asks his dad, "Aren't method actors the ones that go crazy? Get too deep in their role?"

"Hope not," Jerry says.

The wind slams the door shut behind them.

At that, Roberta takes off her coat and claps her hands. "Now? Who's for cookies?"

Natalie smiles up at me, a shining gleam in her eyes.

"You are diabolical," I say.

She nods, grinning. "Merry Christmas."

25

NATALIE

GABE DRAGS ME DOWN THE HALL, HIS FEET POUNDING ON the floor. I hurry after him, my arm stretched, as he storms toward the bedroom.

Back in the kitchen I can hear my mom and grandma arguing about which cookie to bake first—chocolate crinkles or pecan snowballs. Then Grandma says, "I bet that hot actor likes chocolate crinkles. They all like chocolate."

Then Gabe swings open the bedroom door, drags me inside and kicks it shut.

The bedroom was big enough before. Bed. Dresser. Nightstands. Lots of plaid and woodland décor.

Now there isn't room. There's just Gabe.

He fills the space. Taking all the air from the room.

I back against the closed door and then realize my mistake when he cages me in, putting his arms on either side of me. My arm hangs next to his, my back presses against the hard, cool wood of the door. The room is dim, a small spray of light from the north-facing window spills across the carpet but falls short of us.

I lift my chin, try to ignore my pulse storming around my throat, and smile at him.

When he sees my smile his eyes widen, his jaw clenches and he leans even closer, his thighs brushing over mine. His heat licks at me, singes me.

"We need to talk," he says through gritted teeth.

Apparently he wants to have a serious discussion, but I'm having a hard time concentrating on it because my body has decided that being pressed between a door and Gabe's hard body is a really nice place to be.

I stare at his lips only a few inches from mine. They're turned down in a hard frown, but I know for a fact that when he kisses they become soft and warm.

"Let's kiss," I say, moistening my lips.

His eyes turn dark, his pupils dilate, but then he shakes his head and says, "I am not an actor. You cannot tell your family—"

"I already did tell my family—"

"—that I am an actor. I won't continue this farce."

"Then don't. Just kiss me. That's real."

He leans closer, the heat pouring off of him, his thighs pressing into me.

"I want you to tell your family the truth."

"No."

His jaw hardens, and a current passes between us, a struggle between go or stay, kiss or don't. I have the strongest urge to lean forward and bite the juncture where his neck and shoulder meet. I imagine it's salty and sweet and warm.

"You want to spend three days with your family, pretending, playing Christmas?"

"No. I want to spend three more days with you," I say, admitting that it isn't so much about Christmas anymore, that it's about him.

A tortured look passes over his face as he stares down at my lips. His hand, the one cuffed to mine, tangles with my fingers. He clasps our hands together.

"Why?" he asks, voice rough. "Why do you want three more days?"

I look him in the eyes and say, "Because when you kiss me, it feels like Christmas morning."

I barely finish speaking when Gabe's mouth crashes down on mine.

His free hand grabs my hip, his fingers dig into me, and he drags me against him. The thick ridge of him presses into me and I let out a moan. He captures the sound with his mouth.

I bite at his lips, taste his need, drag my hand over his shoulders as he pulls from the door and backs me to the bed.

My knees hit the mattress and I fall onto the bed, Gabe landing over me, his mouth still on mine, his hand holding my hip in place, pressing me down.

I swipe my tongue over his lips and he bites at me, then presses kisses into my mouth, across my jaw, down my neck, to nibble at my pulse. I arch up into him, press against the heat of him.

He sends his hand across my ribs, runs his hands over my breasts. I gasp and he catches the sound with his mouth, pressing his lips to mine. I don't need breath anymore, kissing him is breathing.

The bed creaks under us as he settles more firmly on top of me, lodging himself against me. Everywhere we touch lights like stars winking to life in the night sky.

His fingers brush over my breasts, and when he flicks his thumb over me, a piercing light tumbles through me. I arch into him, plead with him, using kisses and sounds to tell him what I need.

He lifts my sweater, the cool air of the room making goosebumps rise on my skin. His mouth moves over my stomach, up my ribs, I dig my hand into his hair—it's soft and thick—and hold on. He unstraps my bra, one-handed, fast. His mouth captures my breast, and I whimper when his teeth graze me.

I wrap my legs around him, press into him, and find that sensation I've been searching for. The one that feels like a blazing star. A beacon.

I rock into him, and he hums against my breast, sending a vibration down between my legs. He tugs on me, and I arch up, swallow his plea. Then we move, mindless, needing, rocking. There's an ache growing in me, moving in time to the rhythm of his hips and the questing of his lips.

Then he's back at my mouth, his lips wet and hot, and his hand reaches down between us, and just that... just that is enough to have my back bowing, and me crying out into his mouth, as that ache explodes.

When I come down, when I fall back to the soft mattress, feel his body pressed into mine, the hard ridge of him still pressed into me, I turn toward the soft snowflake-light kisses he's spreading over my lips, my jaw, my neck.

Finally he makes his way back up, his mouth on mine, our breath mingling. He looks into my eyes. My cheeks go hot, because he just made me light up with his mouth and the flick of a finger, but also because he's still ready, pressed against me. And I want more. So much more.

"That was nothing like Christmas morning," he says, a low growl in his voice.

"It wasn't?" I look up at him, enjoying the weight of him over me.

He shakes his head. "No. Not at all."

I smile then and say, "I'm glad you liked it."

He smiles back, and I think he's about to start kissing me again, but then there's a knock on the door and Felix shouting, "Natalie? Mom told me to find you. She's baking cookies and we're playing Christmas charades."

"Alright," I shout. Then I look back to Gabe. "Are you ready for this?"

He shakes his head. "I'd rather spend the next three days hiding in here."

He looks so endearing, his hair mussed from my fingers, his cheeks pink and his mouth still glistening from my kisses.

"With me?" I ask.

He fights a smile. "That would be acceptable."

There's another knock. "Natalie?" It's Grandma Agnes. "Gabe? The game is starting, quit hanky pankying and come out here."

His cheeks flush red.

"Coming, Grandma!"

"We could go back to the city," he offers. "I can throw you in a trunk. Tie you to my bed. Doesn't that sound like a nice Christmas?"

There's a low, excited ache in me. But I purse my lips and shove at him. "Maybe next year. Come on. Christmas charades."

As we stand and compose ourselves there's a fiery gleam in Gabe's eyes that makes me wonder how we're going to survive the next three days.

26

GABE

Maybe next year.

Natalie's words echo around my head, clanging around my skull.

Maybe next year.

Those words and the leap I felt in my chest when she said them tell me one thing. This has moved well beyond a hijacked Christmas and a few kisses.

It's no longer about me wanting to avoid all things Christmas and her wanting to tie Christmas lights around my wrists. It's not about Scrooge and Marley or breathing Christmas spirit into my life. It's not even about the evictions or her neighbors.

No.

It's about me and Natalie and the way it feels when I'm near her.

For years I've felt like an empty house, the lights off, the floors unswept, dust gathering on the bookshelves, cobwebs and dust motes covering family photos. The house was closed up years ago and never opened again.

But then Natalie came along, blew open the door in a whirlwind, and swept the dust and cobwebs out. The lights are blazing again. The doors are thrown wide, and a cool, cleansing wind is blowing through.

If I dare, I can invite her in.

Maybe next year.

The thought of next year makes my chest ache. Another Christmas. Another dreaded December. Unless...she's there. Then I don't think I'd dread it. I think I'd look forward to spending it with her.

I shake my head. Unreal.

Natalie smiles up at me, scooting closer on the couch. There's a blaze in the fireplace, Jerry's jostling the logs with a fire poker. They crackle and snap, spitting embers to the chimney. Felix is lounging in the arm chair, ignoring everyone, texting on his phone.

Wait. Phone.

I could call my office, make sure the notices are delivered...

I frown, glance over at Natalie. There's a curious sensation in the pit of my stomach, almost as if I don't want her to be disappointed in me.

Yes, it's my job. Yes, the notices have to be delivered. But...no, there's no buts. I took on this responsibility and I have to follow through.

"Felix. Can I borrow your phone for a minute?"

He glances at me, his elbows on his knees, the phone

sends up a little chirrup as a text comes through. "What? Sure. Just a second."

Natalie elbows me in the side and shakes her head. "No way. No phones."

Roberta strides into the living room, a red platter full of cookies in her hands. "What's this? Felix! You know better. No phones! Hand it over. Sorry, Gabe. We don't do phones around the holidays. It's a family tradition."

"Hang on, Mom. I'm texting work." Felix's fingers fly over the phone, sending three texts in two seconds.

Roberta slides the cookies onto the coffee table. Then holds out her hand, tapping her foot. "Felix."

He sits up straight, his phone chirrups three more times, then he drops his phone into his mom's waiting hands.

"Sorry, Gabe," he says, giving me that stern frown he inherited from his dad. "Mom's rules."

"That's right," Jerry says, setting the fire poker down and wiping his hands. "We don't want any distractions from the spirit of Christmas."

"It'd just be a quick call," I say. Admittedly it's a half-hearted attempt.

"No can do," Roberta says, heading back toward the kitchen. "It's going in the Christmas vault with all the other phones."

I frown at Natalie, and she shrugs, patting my arm. "All phones go in our safe when we come out here. We stopped using them years ago when we realized we were spending more time on our phones than with each other."

That's a nice concept in theory, but in reality? It means that unless I carjack Jerry and Roberta's SUV, I'm spending Christmas with Natalie's family.

"Although I did call the tow truck for you," Jerry says, "Before we locked ours away. Mindy should be here late afternoon, she'll have you fixed up in no time."

"Thanks, Dad." Natalie smiles at him and then rests her hand on my forearm.

I look down at it, then at Natalie. She's smiling at her mom, bringing in a large tray full of steaming mugs. Behind her, Grandma Agnes brings in another plate of cookies. For a moment, I'm almost disappointed that Natalie and I didn't finish decorating our gingerbread men.

Then the smell of freshly baked cookies reaches me, and I think these must be the chocolate crinkles and the pecan snowballs that Natalie's mom and grandma were discussing.

My mouth waters. Natalie did make us lunch, chicken and mashed potatoes, just like she promised, but the sugary smell is too much to resist. I lean forward and grab one of the snowballs, then another, holding it out to Natalie.

She smiles at me. "Thank you."

I shrug then take a bite, the crumbly buttery cookie melting in my mouth. The powdered sugar and pecan are mellow and perfectly balanced.

"What do think?" she asks, popping the cookie in her mouth.

I swallow and lick the sugar from my lips. "Nutty. Just like you."

She hides a laugh. Then she reaches out and grabs a mug with a kitten in a Santa hat and hands it to me. "Hot cocoa with a candied orange chocolate stir stick."

"Are you bribing me to behave?" I ask, taking the steaming mug, the scent of chocolate and orange floating up to me.

"Would it work if I did?" she whispers.

I take a sip of the hot chocolate, the sweet-bitter flavor of the orange and chocolate as rich and luxurious as a set of silk sheets running over bare skin. I stare at Natalie from over the rim of the mug, steam rising, thinking about the silky softness of her skin. How decadent she is.

I set the mug back on the coffee table and nod. "Bribery could work."

Natalie's cheeks flush. The room's growing warm from the heat of the fire.

"Now that is a man that means business," Grandma Agnes says.

Natalie shakes her head and puts some distance between us.

"What happened to that Jason?" Grandma Agnes asks. "Wasn't he supposed to propose?"

"Mom," Roberta hisses.

"Well!" Grandma Agnes throws up her hands. "Everybody's wondering, nobody's asking. She was supposed to come home with one, and here she is with another. Not that I blame her."

Grandma Agnes winks at me and I sit back, raising my eyebrows.

"Jason and I broke up," Natalie says in a light-hearted tone.

Felix scoots forward and grabs two chocolate cookies and a handful of the pecan snowballs. He pops a snowball in his mouth and looks between the two of us, his eyes snagging on the Romeo Football t-shirt I'm wearing. It's his and he knows it.

"Why are you in my clothes?" he asks, starting on another cookie.

"Felix, don't be rude," Roberta says.

"I'm not being rude. It's a fair question."

I glance at Natalie, then back at her brother, "I didn't have time to pack a bag. When you get shoved in a trunk you don't really ask to bring your suitcase along as well."

"Oh. Right," he says, giving me a skeptical look. "What acting school did you go to again?"

"I'm in real estate," I say dryly. "I'm not an actor."

"How did you two meet?" Roberta asks Natalie, trying to steer the conversation in another direction.

Natalie leans forward and says, "I was hired to decorate, he saw my design and we clicked right away."

I lift an eyebrow. Clashed right away is more like it.

"When was that?" Jerry asks. He's brought two more chairs over for Roberta and Agnes. Now everyone is seated in a cozy circle, the fire blazing, the tree lit up, and hot cocoa and cookies spread out before us.

"Yesterday," I say.

Everyone pauses at that, clearly shocked that Natalie

brought a man to her family cabin for Christmas after a one day acquaintance.

"I'm sorry," Grandma Agnes says. "My hearing's going. I thought you said you met Gabe yesterday."

Natalie swallows, her throat bobbing, then she nods. "Uh huh. Yesterday."

Roberta clears her throat, then stands. "Natalie, may I speak with you in the kitchen for a moment?"

Natalie looks over at me, her eyes wide, then back to her mom. "Sure. Okay."

She stands. I stand too.

Roberta's already heading toward the kitchen. We follow, me trailing behind as far as the cuffs allow.

"I told you she has my verve," Agnes whispers after us. "I need to get myself a man like that."

When we make it to the kitchen, Roberta rounds on Natalie her hands on her hips, her lips pursed. "Natalie Giovanna Fiorre, what in heaven's name are—"

She cuts off when she realizes I'm standing only three feet behind her daughter. She blinks quickly, winds back the lecture she was about to unleash like she's winding up a ball of yarn, and then says placidly, "Ah. Gabe. I was hoping to speak to my daughter in private."

Yeah. You and me both.

I hold up my hand, attached to Natalie via the handcuffs. "Sorry."

Roberta narrows her eyes and lets out a sigh. She turns to her daughter. "Natalie, are you able to detach for a moment?" She spins her finger in a circle indicating the leopard print cuffs.

"No. Sorry, Mom."

Her mom frowns between us, clearly taken aback. Maybe she hasn't met her stubborn daughter. I could introduce them.

"Fine. Then I'll just have to say what I'm going to say in front of him. No offense, Gabe."

"None taken," I say, looking at the gingerbread cookies on the nearby counter, wondering if I could reach one. I start to inch my way in that direction when Natalie's mom rounds on her.

"Natalie. What are you thinking? You met this man yesterday and you bring him to a secluded cabin alone? What if he's dangerous? What if he kidnapped you?!"

I snort and then cover it with a cough.

Natalie kicks me in the shin. Of course her mom doesn't notice.

"You're playing fast and loose and I can only think it's because you're heartbroken over Jason. Honey, I know you must be devastated but it isn't the right answer to carry on with the first man you come across. Especially one who...let's face it...he takes this acting thing a little far. It's...odd."

I stop reaching for the gingerbread cookie and frown at Roberta. "I'm not odd. I'm in real estate."

Roberta gives her daughter a look that says, *see, what did I just say, he's odd.*

"Mom." Natalie shakes her head and tugs me back, keeping the gingerbread out of reach. "I'm not heartbroken. I'm fine. Jason and I weren't meant to be. That's all."

Roberta raises a skeptical eyebrow. "Maybe. But that doesn't mean you take up the next day with another man. That's a rebound."

I frown. It doesn't matter that I thought as much yesterday. I don't like hearing it now.

"Sorry, Gabe," Roberta says again.

I wave my hand. "It's fine. Carry on."

I reach again for the cooling rack, to the gingerbread man at the edge. I grasp his leg, the soft cookie in my hands. I haven't had gingerbread in years. And now that the winds are rushing through me, I have the strongest urge to taste it again.

"It isn't like that," Natalie says.

"Then what is it like?" Roberta asks, a challenge in her voice.

I take a bite of the gingerbread man. The flavor explodes in my mouth, I close my eyes and taste the cinnamon, ginger, nutmeg, all that spice mixed with molasses and brown sugar sweetness. It tastes like Natalie, not her addictive flavor, but the spice and the sweet.

I've avoided gingerbread so long, for years, and now I want to gorge on it. Fill myself with it until I can't take any more. I bite off the other leg, the arm, restrain an appreciative moan. This gingerbread is one of the best things I've ever eaten.

"It's..." Natalie pauses. I keep enjoying the delicious

cookie. "It's...Miss Erma called. She told me to bring Gabe home for Christmas."

Mmm. This cookie is out of this world. I bite the last of it, chew, swallow, think about having another.

I open my eyes.

Both Roberta and Natalie are staring at me.

Natalie's smiling but Roberta is looking at me like I'm some long-lost coveted treasure. Which can't be right. I look behind me. No one's there. I look back at them both.

"What?" I ask.

"Miss Erma said you should spend Christmas with us," Natalie says, as if that explains everything.

Apparently to Roberta it does.

"Yes. I know," I say, giving her my *you're cuckoo* look, "That's why I'm here, right?"

"Why didn't you say so?" Roberta says, sliding her arm through mine, pulling me back to the living room. "Jerry, Mother. Natalie says Miss Erma told her to bring Gabe up for Christmas."

Jerry stands then, and all that analytic sharpness fades from his eyes and is replaced by a wistful softness. "She did? Well that's a heck of a thing."

"Really?" Felix asks, tilting his head, giving me a pitying look. "And you're alright with that, Gabe?"

I shrug. "Not really."

"They never are," Grandma Agnes crows.

I have no idea what they're talking about.

Maybe this Miss Erma is always telling women to

clunk men over the head and drag them off to isolated cabins. I'd like to meet this lady, she's a walking lawsuit.

"Well," Jerry says, rubbing his hands together. "See, Roberta? You've been so worried about Natalie, yet here she is with Gabe." He comes over and lightly punches me on the arm. "Good man, good man."

Roberta beams. "Okay. Now that that's settled, let's play charades!"

Natalie and I sit back down on the couch, her thigh pressed to mine, the warmth of the fire settling over us, sending a flickering orange glow across the living room.

I lean close to Natalie, press my mouth against her ear and ask, "Why does Miss Erma matter?"

She gives me an embarrassed look and then whispers apologetically, "They think we're soul mates."

27

NATALIE

GABE HAS A LOT MORE TO SAY, I CAN TELL, BUT HE GAMELY puts it aside for Christmas charades.

Unfortunately, he is, without a doubt, the worst actor in the history of mankind. Apparently, his inability to lie also extends to an inability to act.

We're standing in front of the fireplace, the warmth licking my back, the logs crackling, while Gabe swings his arms in front of him like—

"Tarzan!" Grandma Agnes shouts.

Gabe shakes his head and frowns, rocking his arms faster.

My arm, connected with his, swings in time, yanking back and forth.

"Tarzan and Jane! Tarzan Christmas!" Grandma crows from her armchair.

"It's not Tarzan, Grandma," Felix says, watching Gabe with the look you reserve for a slow-motion train wreck.

Gabe, Grandma, and I are on a team, against Felix, my mom, and my dad. This is the last round, and if we can guess this right, we'll tie for the win. It all comes down to Gabe.

"Swinging…" I say, and Gabe shakes his head no.

"Swinging Christmas!" Grandma yells.

Gabe scowls, the egg timer ticks down. Only sixty seconds left.

My dad and Felix wear identical smug expressions, certain of their win. Usually, I'm on the winning team, so I bet they're enjoying me toppling from my charade tower.

"Try something else," I tell Gabe.

He holds up his pointer finger, frowning at me.

"First word," I say.

He nods. Good.

He balls his hands and puts them to his cheeks and pretends to cry.

"Cry me a river," Grandma shouts. "Cry? Crying? Sad? Blue Christmas!"

Gabe shakes his head no and goes back to rocking his arms and…

"Baby!" I say.

He points at me. Yes!

"Rock the baby Christmas," Grandma says.

"Baby it's Christmas," I say.

Gabe shakes his head no, then starts rubbing his arms and blowing his mouth like a horse.

Grandma hops up from her chair and points at Gabe, "Crying baby horse lips!"

He shakes his head and keeps rubbing his arms, yanking my hand up and down. He blows his lips like you'd blow against a baby's belly.

We have fifteen seconds.

"Baby horse lips for Christmas!" Grandma shouts.

Gabe shakes his head no, his cheeks bright red.

My mom and dad share a look, and Felix mutters, "I guess method acting doesn't mesh with charades."

Gabe looks at me, then he spasms, shaking his arms and legs, and my gosh, he's…

"Tent revival!" Grandma says. "Baby horse tent revival."

"Cold?" I ask and he points at me with a triumphant look in his eyes.

There's five seconds left.

Gabe points at the window.

"Baby cold window…Baby…"

"Baby horse lips on the window!" Grandma yells just as the timer dings.

Gabe drops his head and lets out a strangled, choking noise.

"Well. What was it?" I ask.

He gives me a dry look.

"Baby," he says, rocking his arms, then he shivers, "it's cold"—he points at the window—"outside."

Felix grins at my mom and dad. "Which means we are the champions. Yus!"

He gives Mom and Dad high fives and then grabs a chocolate crinkle from the nearly empty platter.

"Maybe you should look into other fields besides

acting," Grandma says, coming over and patting Gabe's arm in that concerned grandmotherly way she has. "Just in case it doesn't work out."

He stares down at her like he can't believe what he's hearing.

"How about real estate?" he asks dryly.

I give him a side-eye glare. He lifts an eyebrow in response.

"No, you'd be terrible at that. You're too creative, too soft-hearted. My second husband was a realtor—Francis—constant phone calls from stressed out clients, day and night. He suffered terrible insomnia. Never could sleep a wink."

Gabe nods and gives my Grandma a smile, "You're probably right. Sleeping would be a problem."

She pats his arm. "Of course I'm right."

"Don't forget, Natalie," my mom calls as she stacks the mugs onto the tray. "Since you lost, you have kitchen duty."

"What does that mean?" Gabe asks.

"We get to clear the table and do the dishes. Whoever loses at charades over Christmas has to do the dishes for the holiday."

"This is the first time in five years Natalie's had to do the dishes," Felix says with a smug grin. "It's the best Christmas present I've had in years. No dishes." He leans back in his chair, kicks out his feet, and gives a relaxed sigh.

Felix hates doing dishes. Always has.

Gabe leans down then, his mouth hovering next to

my ear, "Are you sure you don't want to go back to the city?"

I shake my head no. Not even if the dishes pile was as tall as Mount Everest.

We're seeing this through to the Christmassy end.

My dad claps his hands. "Who's up for snow shoeing?"

28

GABE

SNOW SHOEING, COOKIE MAKING, A DINNER OF ROASTED ham, cranberries, and yams with carols playing over the stereo.

Natalie's family is full of so much affection for each other. You can see it in the way Roberta feeds her kids every chance she gets, in the way Jerry asks Natalie about her latest decorating projects and listens attentively when she answers, and in the way Agnes pats her grandkids on the arms or pinches their cheeks jokingly whenever she passes them. Even Felix manages to tease Natalie with good-natured brotherly fondness.

At first, standing in the midst of so much affection left a raw, scraping sort of feeling.

But then, when Roberta handed me a gingerbread man covered in icing, and Jerry asked where I grew up, and Felix asked if I liked hiking or climbing—because he could show me some places in the spring—the raw feeling faded and was replaced by incredulity.

Is this what a family is?

I glance over at Natalie, she's quietly humming "Jingle Bells"—badly—the lights of the kitchen gleaming off her pink cheeks.

Steam rises from the kitchen sink and the clank of silverware and plates is loud. My hand moves with hers in the hot water, the bubbles up past my wrist. She's scrubbing a plate with a washcloth, and when she's done she hands it to me.

I take the clean plate, rinse it, then put it in the drying rack.

"We might get a dishwasher one of these years," she says, nudging me with her arm and smiling.

"But then there wouldn't be a prize for winning charades," I say, taking the next plate she hands me.

She hums an ascent and then rubs her forehead with her sleeve, wiping the sheen from the steam off her skin. Her chestnut curls have gone wild from the humidity and they surround her like a halo.

It's late. Nearly eleven. Everyone else is in bed, promising an early morning of ornament decorating and pine cone collecting. Felix volunteered to sleep on the pull-out couch in the living room. I can hear his snoring even with the kitchen door closed.

Natalie hands me a cluster of forks and spoons, I take them and rinse them off.

"What's with the soul mate thing?" I ask, noting her cheeks turning a darker shade of red when I do.

"Oh you know." She shrugs. "Romeo's famous for soul mates. Miss Erma can see who's meant to be. My parents were matched by her. If she tells you your soul mate, that's it, you'll be together for the rest of your lives. It's a pretty big deal around here."

"So she's a matchmaker?" I ask, taking another plate.

"No. Nothing like that. She can just tell. She sees it. If she said to me, Natalie, your soul mate is Gabe Cavanaugh, then that'd be it. You and me, done."

I raise an eyebrow. "Really? Just like that."

She nods, the dishes clank together, and my hand dips further into the hot water as she reaches for another dish.

"Just like that." She scrubs away, and the soap bubbles tickle my arm. "My mom was so worried when I moved away. But Miss Erma assured me—"

"You'd find a Christmas-loving man?"

I remember what she said earlier.

Natalie nods and hands me a white ceramic serving dish to rinse. I run the water over it then place it on the rack. It's almost full of dishes.

"I have a present for him," she says quietly.

I look at her quickly. "Who?"

"My soul mate," she says, looking down into the soap bubbles.

"You know who it is?" I frown. Whoever he is, I don't like him.

"No. I don't know," she says, swishing the water around. "Do you like your job?" she asks suddenly.

I reach around Natalie, take a pan from the counter

and drop it into the sink. It kerplunks and bubbles fly up then settle back down, their purple, blue and green iridescence flashing.

"I like it well enough," I say. "My grandfather started the company. My dad and uncle continued it. Now there's me."

"Is it all evictions all the time?" she asks, her eyebrows raised archly. "Generations of scrooges?"

"No." I scoot her over and dip both hands into the sink, scrubbing at the pan. "When my grandfather first started the company he was strictly in residential rentals. But my dad and uncle expanded so that we tore down old buildings and put in new ones."

She makes an unhappy noise.

I take the pan and rinse it off, then reach for the last pan on the counter.

"It's not as bad as it sounds. Sometimes we put up buildings with hundreds of units instead of the twenty that were there before. It means more people can live in the city. Sometimes we build family homes, beautifully constructed. Think of it, we tear buildings down, but we also put something beautiful back up."

I know she's thinking of Hudson Apartments. So am I. In this case, it isn't as clear cut.

We're gearing to create a showpiece townhouse for a corporate investor, it'll be the way-station for their traveling executives. But to be honest, the more time I spend with Natalie, the less I want to continue down the Hudson Apartment tear-down path.

"That all sounds so reasonable," Natalie says. "Tear

down the small and the old to create something beautiful and big. Unless you're the one losing your home."

I frown, her censure makes me shift on my feet, "Twenty units that can become two hundred. What about the people who will make the building their new home?"

It's her turn to shift on her feet, then she frowns up at me. "Don't make me think about it. If there are shades of gray, I'll start to feel bad about bringing you here. I'll feel terrible if you aren't really a scrooge."

I smile at her. "No. I'm a scrooge. Don't worry. I'm as black-hearted as they come. Bah humbug."

I reach into the sink, scoop up a handful of soap bubbles, and wipe them across her nose.

She sputters, her mouth falls open, and because she looks so ridiculous covered in bubbles I laugh. Her eyes narrow, she grabs bubbles and smears them on my jaw and my cheeks.

The bubbles are light, warm, and soft.

Natalie grins at me, the bubbles still on her nose. "Why Santa! You are real! I always believed!"

In the window over the sink I see my reflection. Sure enough, I have a snowy white bubble beard.

I snort. Then I'm scooping up more bubbles, and so is Natalie, and we're throwing them at each other, and she's laughing and bubbles are flying through the air, and I feel just as free, so free that I grip Natalie's hips, pick her up, push her onto the counter, and take her mouth in mine.

The bubbles pop, our mouths are slick, and she laughs against my lips.

"I've got it," she says.

"What?" I ask, nibbling at her mouth.

"I saw mommy kissing Santa Claus. We would've won if we had that one."

"Natalie?"

"Hmmm?"

"I'm ready to call in my favor."

I HAVE TO ADMIT, WHEN GABE SAID HE WANTED TO CALL IN his favor I practically melted against him, ready for whatever he wanted.

My lips were tingling, the kitchen was spinning, and visions of sugary icing and licking danced in my head.

Now. Not so much.

He wanted a shower, a toothbrush, bed. If I'd thought it was difficult going to the bathroom handcuffed together, it's even more difficult showering.

My arm extends to the shower curtain. Gabe's naked behind it. There's the sound of the water sliding over him, the scent of peppermint soap, clean and bright. Steam curls through the room, rising like mist over the pine tree wallpaper.

To start he'd stepped into the shower and pulled the curtain. The rings screeched against the metal and the curtain billowed. There was a zip. The rustling of clothes removed. Then he dropped his jeans to the white tile floor. Then his boxers. Then his t-shirt came down his arm and looped around mine. And that was that.

Three feet and a curtain separates us.

The noise of the shower is soothing, the steam relaxing, but visions of sugar icing and licking have been replaced with the reality of Gabe's forearm, extending past the shower curtain, water sluicing down his tanned skin.

A water drop slides down the corded lines of his forearm, trailing down to his wrist, settling like a dew drop on a flower petal. I have the strongest urge to lean forward and lick the water off his skin.

I close my eyes.

The sound of the shower stops, the rainlike noise trickling to quiet. Now there's only the hum of the fan and my shallow breaths.

"Natalie?" Gabe says, his voice quiet.

"Hmmm?"

"Can you hand me a towel?"

Right. I hurriedly grab the fluffy hunter green towel on the rack and thrust it past the curtain.

"Thank you." He takes it and then pulls the curtain aside.

I catch a glimpse of hard abs, wide shoulders, the corded muscles of an athlete. My gaze dips to the flat lines of his abdomen. A dusting of dark hair leads down to the edge of the towel slung low over his hips. I turn away quickly.

"Are you going to take one?" he asks, bending down to grab his clothing.

"Yes," I say, jumping into the shower and pulling the curtain shut.

A cold shower.

His laugh rolls over me and ignites me with fiery heat.

Make that a freezing cold shower.

THE BEDROOM IS DARK, THE BED WARM, THE SMELL OF peppermint soap strong. My mouth is minty from the toothpaste and my lips tingle.

Gabe's breathing is soft and even. The blanket rests over us like a warm cloud trapping our heat, making the bed cozy and soft. The clock on the nightstand shines with fluorescent blue block numbers stating that it's 11:49.

I lie on my back, my hand pressed to Gabe's, our fingers barely touching.

You could say that the touch is accidental, except neither of us is pulling away. All my concentration is on the small point of skin where my pointer meets his ring finger, where his pinkie touches mine. My breath is short, my lungs unable to bring in enough air.

Who knew that a millimeter of skin, the heat of a ring finger could make me come undone? Who knew that the scent of peppermint could be an erotic prelude?

"Tell me something about yourself," Gabe says, his low rumble quiet in the dark.

My hand flutters, like a startled butterfly. He drags his fingers over mine and I still beneath him.

"What do you want to know?" I say quietly.

He turns toward me, the blanket shifting over my skin, and I shiver at the sensation. My legs are bare expect for a pair of pajama shorts. I'm in the same cashmere sweater I've been in all day. Unfortunately, we haven't figured out how to change out of shirts while handcuffed.

"I know the basics," he says, his pointer running down my ring finger, drawing a sharp exhale from me. "You love Christmas. You love your family. And...you love kidna—"

"Hey! Unfair!" Then I think about it for a second and say, "Actually, I am enjoying being tied to you."

He makes a scoffing noise. His eyes shine in the moonlight though, and the way he's looking at me feels like he's wrapping me in his arms, holding me tight.

"I was terrified to leave home," I tell him. "I've never told anyone that, especially not my family. They were already so worried about me leaving Romeo. I was scared I'd fail and have to come back home. At the same time, I was scared I'd succeed and never be able to come back home. I was terrified that leaving—even though I wanted to—meant that when I came back, it wouldn't be home anymore."

"Is that what happened?" he asks. He reaches up and brushes my curls back from my face.

I nod. "I was so lonely. I cried sometimes, but when my parents called and said they missed me I told them I was happy, that I was building my dream. And I did it. I built a successful business, I made friends, and I made a community—sort of like a family—in the building I live in."

Gabe's lips turn down and his hand stills, no longer tracing over mine. But he starts again almost right away and says, "Your family's proud of you."

"They are." I smile. "Nobody thought a business that decorates for the holidays was a good idea, but it's been so successful. I have two warehouses full to the brim, a company moving van, year-round clients for all the holidays. Not just Christmas, but New Year's, Valentine's Day, Easter, the Fourth of July, the list goes on. I did it. You know? I went out into the cold, even though back home it was warm and safe and cozy, and I survived. I made it. And I know my mom has been worried that I'd never find my soul mate, but..."

"You found me instead," Gabe says, a wry note in his voice.

"Alas, if only you loved Christmas." I scoot over the sheets, move closer and smile into his eyes, the pepperminty smell stronger now.

"If only," he says, the warmth of his lips so close. He brushes his mouth over mine and the night grows full, expectant.

"If you could choose one moment to live again—only one, from your whole life—which would you choose?" I ask, reaching up and running my hand over the stubble growing on his jaw.

"None. I like my life." His face closes off, the dark of the room shadowing him again.

I send my fingers over his jaw, tracing the roughness there. He turns his head and presses his mouth into my palm. His lips are warm, his mouth gentle, he sucks on the flesh of my hand and I make a quiet noise. Gabe's eyes flame as he looks at me.

"What about you?" he asks, pressing another kiss into my palm.

I want to tell him—*right now. I'd live this moment again. Right here. Right now.*

Instead I say what would've been true before I met him. "I'd go back to when I was a kid. Five years old. Christmas morning. I still believed in Santa. I'd run down the stairs, practically flying from the excitement. There was so much magic. The tree was glowing. There was a huge present wrapped in gold paper—the playhouse I'd asked Santa for—and I was so happy I thought I was going to burst. My mom made Christmas cinnamon rolls. My dad lit a fire and sang "Jingle Bells." Felix got the toboggan he wanted and he let me ride with him down the hill in our backyard. I still remember how my stomach felt when we sped down that hill. Like I'd left it at the top and it was trying to catch up with me. Then we came in and had hot cocoa and played Christmas charades with my mom and dad and had our Christmas cake. I found the star in the cake that year, so I got to make the wish. I still remember it. I wished that every Christmas would be just as happy."

"Have they been?" he asks.

I nod, pressing my pointer to his lips. "So far."

He takes my finger in his mouth, nips at my skin. "I changed my mind," he says then, kissing the tip of my finger. "I'd go back too. I'd relive Christmas Eve when I was seven. You're right. That's the thing to do."

I smile at him. "You still loved Christmas when you were seven?"

"I did."

I reach out, lace my hand with his. "If you loved it once, you could love it again. The magic is always there, sometimes we just forget how to see it."

"The world can be a cold, dark place," he says, brushing his lips over mine, making sparks dance across my eyes.

"Then come inside," I whisper.

At that, Gabe takes my mouth.

I love his kisses. I love his mouth on mine. This time though, we don't stop at kissing.

I reach out and tug the button of his jeans free. I shove at them, struggle to pull them down. He tries to help. Our hands tangle, the cuffs clank. I keep kissing him, dragging his jeans down. Our hands jerk again, the handcuffs stopping us from doing what we want to do.

Gabe lets out a low curse. Then kicks off his jeans. My eyes widen. He's long and hard. I lean down, grasp him by his length. He's smooth and fiery hot. I grip him and run my hand up him, then down. He makes a harsh noise deep in his throat. I lean down and kiss him on his tip.

His free hand clasps the blanket.

I put my mouth around him, swirl my tongue. He makes a desperate, harsh sound.

He pulls me free of him, takes my cheek in his hand and rubs his hand over my lips.

"Natalie," he says, his voice strained and rough. "Take off the handcuffs."

It's a demand. A promise.

"Now?" I ask. I lick my lips and his length jerks in response.

"Now."

30

GABE

THE KEYS WERE IN HER JEANS POCKET, WHICH WERE NEATLY folded on the dresser.

I'm too far gone to think about the fact that all this time the key was inches away. I could've easily obtained it if I'd searched her. I could've been free if I wanted. It's time to admit that I haven't wanted to be free. Even if she gave me my phone and the keys to a car, I'd stay.

I'm not tied up with Christmas lights or handcuffs anymore. I'm tied up in her.

She turns the small silver key, her hand shaking. Then the cuffs fall free. They clank to the floor, thudding on the carpet.

The weight of the metal is gone, and suddenly I can do everything I want to do.

We're standing at the foot of the bed, the tension crackles between us. Natalie opens her hand and drops the key to the floor.

Then she leans forward, her curls falling around her face, her smile hesitant and questioning.

She's worried. Maybe she thinks that I'll take this opportunity to leave.

Not a chance.

"I'm going to unwrap you like a present," I promise.

At that her hesitant smile vanishes and is replaced by a look of desire that I imagine matches my own.

She steps forward, takes my shirt and lifts it over my head. I barely feel the cool room air. I'm burning standing this close to her. Then she presses her hand to my heart and brushes her lips across my naked chest.

I close my eyes.

Her mouth is so hot, the touch of it almost hurts. I'm barely able to control myself.

I take her red cashmere sweater, untie the fabric belt looped around her waist.

"There goes the bow," she whispers as I drop it to the floor.

I tug the sweater over her head and let it fall. Then I caress her lace bra, feel the weight of her breasts in my hands. And as she draws in a breath, her breasts rise.

I lean down and put my mouth to her, suck her through the lace of her bra. She tastes like mint and cookies. Slowly I unsnap her bra, let it fall free.

She's beautiful. Her breasts are full, her nipples rosy, her stomach curving to her hips. Even in the dark I can see the flush spreading from her cheeks to her breasts. It's the red of candy canes. I want to taste her everywhere.

I rub my thumbs along her hips, then ever so slowly I push her shorts down her thighs. She isn't wearing anything under the shorts. She's bare before me.

"All unwrapped," she whispers.

I smile, letting her see how much I want her. She reaches forward, grips my length. I hiss at the pressure of her hand around me.

Then I pick her up and toss her onto the mattress. She smirks at me. It's that same mischievous smile she wore when I fell out of her trunk.

I wanted to kiss her then. Now I want to do more.

I bend down, grab the handcuffs off the floor. "I'm cuffing you to the bed and then I'm going to lick you until you come undone. Try not to scream."

"Turnabout's fair play?"

"That's right." I smile, settle the cuff around her wrist, loop the metal through the slats of the headboard and lock her in place.

The comforter pools around her, soft and warm. I kneel at the foot of the bed then kiss my way up her legs. At her thighs, I run my hands over her curves, and she rises toward me, letting out a small, needy sound. I press a kiss against her and hold her down.

"Please," she whispers.

I send my fingers into her, nearly exploding at the tight heat of her. Then I kiss her, taste her, and marvel at how sweet she is.

She lifts to me, moves with my mouth and my hand. And then she's crying out, trying her best to stay quiet. I feel her tightening around my fingers. I kiss her again, then rise up, look at the flush in her cheeks and the need in her eyes and unlock the handcuffs.

At that she pulls me on top of her and guides me to the core of her. I rest between her legs, wait for her. She tilts her hips up, sending me a half-inch, an inch into her. I let out a harsh breath at the heat of her, the warmth.

"Now?" I ask.

"Now," she says.

I thrust into her.

I bury myself in her and the world lights up. It's not cold anymore. It's not dark. It's bright and warm and light is everywhere. She makes a noise, grabs my lips with her own. Then we're moving. I can't stay still. I have to move. Every time I withdraw I miss her and so I have to come inside her again.

She wraps herself around me, whispers words against my mouth. Holds me close. I can't stop. I don't want to stop. I want to keep doing this forever.

"Natalie. Natalie." I'm murmuring her name, moving with her.

She tastes like peppermint, like gingerbread, like Christmas.

If Natalie tastes like Christmas, if Natalie is my Christmas, then I love Christmas. I'll love it for the rest of my life.

Her fingernails drag down my back, her heels dig into me, her mouth captures mine.

And when I reach down to stroke her, and feel her

tightening around me, the world blazes bright, like the star on top of the tree.

She cries out, takes me deeper, pulses around me.

With that, I thrust into her and lose myself.

For a blissful moment I...love.

31

NATALIE

DECEMBER 23, 7:41 AM

THE SMELL OF CINNAMON, NUTMEG, ORANGE AND cranberries teases me out of sleep. Mmm. Cranberry orange muffins.

They'll be tender, sweet, with a dusting of cinnamon sugar on top.

I smile and then stretch, burrowing a little deeper against Gabe. My leg is thrown over his. My head rests in the space between his shoulder and chest. My hands rest on his abdomen.

He's warm, solid. Here.

"Morning," he says, his voice sleep-filled and rough.

"Good morning." I close my eyes, a little afraid to look at him.

We're naked. I'm wrapped around him like a ribbon on a Christmas present, but I'm afraid to look into his eyes.

Last night we made love, then we made love again, and then around four a.m. Gabe woke me up with a kiss and we made love again.

I'm not going to call it anything other than what it was. We were making love.

Something inside me opened up and every joy, every happiness, every Christmas morning I've had, it all faded in comparison to what I felt in Gabe's arms. What I'm feeling right now.

Which is terrifying.

Because let's face it, we've only known each other for two days, and Gabe isn't here because he wants to be.

So I'm scared to look in his eyes. I'm afraid that I'll see that last night didn't mean anything. Or that he can't wait to leave. Because when Christmas is over all of this will end.

"What is it?" Gabe asks, taking a lock of my hair and looping it around his finger.

"What do you mean?" I tuck my face against his chest and let his warmth sink into my cheek. I settle into the mattress, memorize the heat of him, the dusting of hair, his long limbs tangled with mine.

"You were relaxed and now you're not. You're all tense and scrunchy." He tugs on my lock of hair, the curl smooths out and then springs back.

"Hmmph." I make a noncommittal noise. "What is scrunchy?"

"Your muscles are tense. Your hands are balled. Are you regretting—"

"No." I look up quickly.

"—the handcuffs." He grins at me.

At his smile all the fear that had locked itself around my heart falls away. His eyes are clear, warm, happy. They remind me of a sunny, cozy morning at the cabin, with bright snow, a warm fire, and a day full of endless possibilities ahead.

I press my hand into his chest, sit up and let the sheet fall off my shoulder, the cool air brushing over me. I peer down at him.

His morning stubble is dark, his hair is messy, and his warm smell, peppermint and loving wraps around me. He reaches up and brushes my hair back from my face, tucking it behind my ear.

My heart picks up speed. "I thought you'd want to leave," I admit.

He makes a surprised noise, his hand coming round my back, pressing me down on top of him. I can feel him ready beneath me.

"Why would I want to do that?"

Then he proceeds to show me how much he wants to stay.

Two cranberry orange Christmas muffins and a cup of coffee later, Gabe and I are in the kitchen, ready to unroll the little slip of paper from the advent calendar.

"This tradition goes back to my ancestors," Grandma Agnes says, dimpling at Gabe.

She thinks he's strapping. I know this because she cornered me when I came out of the bathroom this morning and told me to tie this hunky strapping man up before he got away.

If she only knew.

"Really?" Gabe asks, giving Grandma his full attention.

I smile at him, completely taken aback by his transformation. He's in another pair of old borrowed jeans and a T-shirt, one that says *I went to Romeo and all I got was my soul mate.*

He took a shower this morning, his hair is still tousled and slightly damp. He didn't shave though, his stubble's growing in, and he has a carefree, relaxed expression. He looks years younger. He looks as if a heavy weight has been lifted.

He sees me watching him and sends me a quick smile, there then gone. He turns back to my grandma.

She's fluffing her short white curls, "Yes indeed. My ancestors brought the advent scrolls over on the *Mayflower.*"

"Mother," my mom strides into the kitchen, bringing in my dad's coffee mug to refill. "Your ancestors came over from Italy in 1938. Stop confusing poor Gabe."

"No, no," Grandma says, giving me a wink. "They came over on the *Mayflower.* But they hated Plymouth so much that they sailed for Sicily instead. My goodness, those Puritans were something else. Did you know they banned Christmas? True story! They banned it! Of course my ancestors left."

My mom lets out a long sigh, and refills my dad's snowflake mug. My grandma likes to stretch the truth. My mom says she stretches it, twists it, and then turns it upside down. Either way, it's always fun to listen to her stories.

"They banned it?" Gabe asks with interest.

Felix wanders into the kitchen, grabs a fresh muffin from the serving platter on the table and takes a bite. "Grandma, are you telling the Puritan story again?"

She reaches over and pinches Felix's cheek. He pulls out a chair and sits, resting his elbows on the table. He's still in his flannel pajamas, so he looks just like he did when he was a little kid, devouring muffins, listening to Grandma tell stories at breakfast.

"Sure am. Gabe here doesn't know about the Puritans. It's a lesson, this one. It's called don't ban Christmas."

"Scrooge did that, didn't he?" asks Gabe, sending me a sly look.

"No, no," Grandma says, waving that away. "It's the Puritans that did it. They did it in Massachusetts and they did it in Britain. They banned Christmas, feasting, presents, good cheer, gathering together, they forbade it all. You couldn't even take the day off. If you were found with your family gathering to celebrate Christmas you were fined or put in the stocks! That's why my ancestors hopped on a boat and went to Italy. They knew how to celebrate Christmas there."

"Why'd they ban it?" Felix asks, devouring another muffin.

Grandma tsks. "They thought it was sinful. Christmas, make-up, sports, dancing, carols, feasting, all sorts of things were banned. They had soldiers roaming the streets, just looking for people disobeying their silly rules. Those Puritans went out of favor quickly. If you want to stay in power, don't ban Christmas. They didn't know that in the 1600s."

"Don't believe anything she says," my mom says, pouring cream into my dad's coffee.

"It's all true," my grandma says, "nearly almost every bit of it."

I cover a laugh.

My mom shakes her head, then sees the roll of paper in Gabe's hand. "Gabe, you're claiming today's advent?" She sounds surprised and pleased.

"Looks like it."

"We're doing it together," I say.

"Let's see what it is." Grandma scoots closer.

Gabe unrolls the piece of paper to find my mom's scrolling calligraphy. "What does it say?"

He looks at me, an amused expression on his face. "Deliver Christmas cookies to the retirement center. Sing carols to the residents."

"You'll need a car," Felix says.

"Natalie's will be fixed by this afternoon," my dad

calls from the living room. "Mindy called to say she'll bring it by."

We have a car.

We're leaving the cabin.

We're going into Romeo.

Gabe gives me a delighted grin.

32

GABE

ROMEO, NEW YORK IS WHAT EVERY NEW YORKER DREAMS of when they're imagining that Upstate vacation away from the stress of the city.

The downtown looks as if a gang of elves flew down from the North Pole and smacked the whole place with lights, garlands, red velvet bows, and giant candy canes.

Natalie's driving down Main Street, giving me the unofficial tour as we head toward the retirement center.

On the left we have a chocolate shop with a life-size chocolate gingerbread house in the window. There's a bookstore with a six-foot-tall Christmas tree made from stacked books and strung up with lights. The hardware store has a row of Christmas trees out front, ready for those who waited until the last minute. There are people chatting on the street, bags of gifts in their arms.

On the right, we pass the town park, where there are ice sculptures of nutcrackers, reindeer and Santa's sleigh. There's a bronze statue with a Santa hat. Kids in brightly colored snowsuits are building a snowman. There's a wooden hot cocoa stand at the edge of the park.

If I had to find a town to film one of those TV Christmas movies in, this would be it.

This town loves Christmas.

"Why'd you leave again? This town is perfect for you." I look over at Natalie, she's bundled in her coat and scarf, her cheeks pink from the cold. Her car heater still hasn't warmed up. It's blowing cold air over us.

"You know, small town girl, big city dreams." She smiles at me, but it's a little less vibrant than it was last night.

"Ah. That's right. Well, it looks like a nice place to grow up."

"The best."

It's late afternoon. We spent the day painting salt clay ornaments with Roberta, cross country skiing with Felix and Jerry, and then baking the cookies with Agnes for the retirement center.

The smell of the sugar cookies—butter and sugar and vanilla—fills the car. Grandma Agnes claimed it's an old family recipe, to which Natalie pointed to the recipe on the side of the flour bag and winked at me.

But even with that wink, and spending all day together, I've noticed Natalie's smiles spacing out and her confidence waning. Even now her knuckles are white on the steering wheel and I don't think it has to do with the cold.

"You're worried that I'll go back to the city," I say, reaching over and brushing my hand over her fingers.

She glances at me then back to the road. We've made it to the turn off for the retirement center. The tires crunch over the salt on the driveway. Ahead, the front doors are wrapped like Christmas presents, and there are lights in the windows.

She pulls into a parking spot and puts the car in park, but leaves the engine running. The heater has finally started to send out heat.

"I'm not going to lie," she says. "I'm fairly certain we're going to walk in there, you're going to ask to use the phone, and then five minutes later a car is going to show up to drive you back to the city."

"The thought did cross my mind."

Her hands grip the steering wheel tighter and she arranges her features like a man facing a long march to the gallows.

I brush my hand over her jaw. She turns to me.

"I'm not sorry," she whispers.

"I don't want you to be sorry."

She turns her face into my palm. "Good. Because I'd do it again."

The warmth from the heater curls around me and I run my thumb along her jaw, stroke her cheek.

I want to kiss her. I crave her. I want to nibble on her mouth like she's a sugar cookie covered in icing. Even after last night and all the kisses I stole today, the craving isn't lessening, it's getting stronger.

"If I call for a car," I tell her, leaning over the box of cookies, pressing my mouth to the corner of her lips.

She frowns and I kiss her again, trying to iron the frown away.

"If you call for a car?"

I kiss her again, tasting the sugar cookie on her lips.

I'd forgotten where I was going with this. Ah, now I remember.

"I'd have to tie you up and chuck you in the back seat of the car. Force you back to the city with me. But that would result in awkward questions from the driver and your family would get upset. I like your family. I don't want them to get upset."

Her frown has cleared, replaced by a slow smile. "It would be a shame to upset the driver. And my family."

"It would," I agree. "It would be a terrible shame."

We stare at each other, the air in the car as electrified as a string of Christmas lights. Natalie picks up the box of cookies, her eyes as green as a balsam fir.

"Let's go deliver these cookies," she says, biting her bottom lip. I want to taste her again. "You can meet Miss Erma."

I lift my eyebrows. "The kidnapping mastermind."

Natalie laughs, "No. The woman who predicts soul mates. Come on, you'll like her."

Thinking about what she said about Natalie's soul mate—that he's not me—I'm not so sure I will.

33

NATALIE

MISS ERMA IS IN THE COMMUNITY ROOM LEADING A Christmas craft class.

The room is a large, rectangular open space with lots of windows that let in the bright winter light.

To the left is a catering kitchen where smells of coffee and fresh cinnamon rolls punches the air. To the right there are a dozen round tables piled with craft supplies.

The place is packed. At each of the tables residents of the center and their families—kids, grandkids, great-grandkids—paint ornaments, craft wreaths, and pour glitter into mason jars for homemade snow globes.

I know nearly everyone here. Which isn't surprising, Romeo is a small town where people go out of their way to stay in touch and help each other out.

And at one table there's Chloe Daniels, her husband Nick O'Shea—they were two years ahead of me in school—and their daughter. I'm not surprised to see them, Miss Erma is Chloe's great-aunt.

Chloe runs a greeting card company with her best friend Veronica. It looks like she's helping kids make Christmas cards for their grandparents while Nick entertains their daughter by holding mistletoe over her head and giving her raspberry kisses.

Every time he waves the mistletoe she giggles and he blows a kiss on her cheek. I bet she's only about a year old, but she clearly has Nick wrapped around her little finger.

When Chloe sees me she gives me a wide smile and waves.

Usually when I come up for holidays, we'll catch up over coffee and cookies. When I started my business I asked her and Veronica for advice, they steered me in the right direction in terms of business plans, business accounts, and contracts.

I wave back, mouthing hi, then a little boy tugs on Chloe's sleeve, pointing his paintbrush at his card. Chloe gives me another wave and then bends down to help the little boy.

"Hi Natalie!" Wanda calls from the wreath table, a battery-powered hot glue gun in her hand.

"Hi Wanda." I wave and keep pulling Gabe through the tables toward the front of the room.

"Do you know everyone here?" he asks, looking around with a slight frown on his face.

"Just about. It's what happens when you grow up in

the same tiny town where your parents grew up and where your grandparents grew up. You know everyone."

"I wonder what they'd say if they knew about your Christmas crime."

I look around at the festivity, "I think they would've helped me tie you up."

He nods. "Probably."

I smile and then gesture at the front of the room. "Come on."

"Deck the Halls" plays over the sound system, adding to the din of chatting and laughter.

At the front, Miss Erma stands at a rectangular table demonstrating how much glitter to add to the mason jar. A little girl in a green velvet dress stands on her chair at a table nearby and watches Miss Erma with rapt attention, then she dumps about a cup of glitter into her jar.

"Very good, Evangeline!" Miss Erma says, her voice rising over the carols.

It's then Miss Erma catches Gabe and me walking through the tables to the front of the room.

Gabe's carrying the large white bakery box full of three dozen sugar cookies. I have a bag full of Christmas cards from my mom to hand out to everyone.

"Natalie!" Miss Erma smiles and steps out from behind the table. "Merry Christmas!"

"Merry Christmas, Miss Erma," I say, bending down to give her a hug.

Miss Erma is barely five feet tall. She's a fine-boned, tiny powerhouse. She's in her eighties but she has more energy than most toddlers. I've been in awe of her since I was small, listening to my parents' story of how she matched them over Christmas.

If you stay in Romeo for more than an hour or two, you'll meet someone who will tell you all about Miss Erma. She sees soul mates and now that I'm here, I realize I want her to take one look at Gabe and say, *that's him, he's your soul mate.*

Miss Erma gives me a squeeze, the scent of Darjeeling tea floating around her. She takes a step back and looks me over. "You look well. Are you enjoying your job at the pizza parlor?"

I shake my head. "Miss Erma, I don't work at the pizza place. I'm a decorator. In New York."

She clasps my hand. "Oh good. I'm glad. I told Wanda you shouldn't quit your dream. It suits you."

"Thank you." I smile, then nod at Gabe. "This is Gabe Cavanaugh. Gabe, this is Miss Erma."

Her eyes light up when she sees him. A bright look enters her brown eyes, she looks from Gabe, to me, then back to Gabe.

There's a pounding noise in my ears and I realize it's my heart. My mouth goes dry, waiting...waiting for Miss Erma to say something.

"Nice to meet you," Gabe says, shifting the box of cookies to one hand and reaching out to shake Miss Erma's hand.

She takes his hand in both of hers and squeezes. "Gabe Cavanaugh," she says, her lips pursing. "I heard you're a scrooge."

I flush in embarrassment.

Gabe's eyebrows lift. "And I heard you told Natalie her soul mate loves Christmas," Gabe joins Miss Erma in eschewing small talk.

Miss Erma laughs, pulling her red shawl around her shoulders. "Yes. I did, didn't I?"

Gabe frowns, then asks, "Have you ever been wrong?"

They stare at each other. Gabe, a tall man who looks as if he's forgotten his spine can bend. Miss Erma, a tiny woman who is larger than life.

Miss Erma tilts her head, her eyes cloud, sifting through the past, through the hundreds of matches she's foretold. She lifts a shoulder. "Once."

I blink. This is one of those moments where the music should scratch and the entire room should descend into silence. But "All I Want For Christmas Is You" continues to play and all the people continue to laugh and craft.

I'm stunned though. This moment is like someone telling you the sun rises in the west not the east, or that the sky is green, not blue. It can't possibly be true. Miss Erma has never been wrong. That's legend. That's fact.

"So you could be wrong," Gabe says, going after that *once* like a dog after a bone.

She shakes her head. "No. I'm not wrong. You'll see."

But she was once.

Why? How?

"You brought cookies?" Miss Erma asks Gabe, gesturing toward the box.

"Sugar cookies," I say. "Three dozen. They're for everyone."

Miss Erma pats Gabe's arm, "Be a dear, go ahead and drop them in the kitchen."

Gabe has manners, so instead of staying to ask more questions, he nods politely and murmurs, "Of course. It was a pleasure meeting you."

Miss Erma watches him go, a small smile on her face.

"Once?" I say when Gabe is out of earshot.

She turns back to me, her gaze shrewd. "In 1948. We don't talk about that year." She waves it away and levels me with a direct stare. "What did you want to know?"

I swallow nervously, watch Gabe slip into the kitchen. I only have thirty seconds tops before he returns.

"Me and Gabe?" I ask, lacing my fingers together, praying for an affirmative.

Miss Erma pats my arm. "I already told you all I know, dear. You know what to do."

I nod.

I do.

"Do you still have it?" Miss Erma asks.

"Yes."

"Good. Then there's no reason to worry."

Then the little girl, Evangeline, is taking Miss Erma's hand, asking her to come see her snow globe, and Gabe is back, his presence warm and welcome.

"What now?" he asks, frowning after Miss Erma.

I heft the bag in my hand. "We deliver Christmas cards and sing carols."

"And then?" he asks, searching my gaze.

I want to step into his arms, find a hidden alcove and kiss him. "Then...we'll start a new Christmas tradition."

His eyes light up. "Will I like it?"

"I hope so."

I'm hinging my future on it.

NATALIE

I PULL THE CAR TO A STOP AT THE ROADSIDE OVERLOOK midway between the town of Romeo and our cabin.

The narrow country road that leads to our cabin winds through the quiet northern woods, tracking along the mountain.

In the summer the woods are a cool, jewel-green haven full of chirping wood thrush, tittering squirrels, and the occasional black bear snuffling the wild raspberry bushes that thrive at the woodland's edge.

But in winter these woods are still, the evergreens hold the thick snow in their arms, like a mother cradling a child, hushing the forest into a quiet winter sleep. I love the woods in winter.

"There's an overlook just through there," I tell Gabe, parking in the crescent drive looping off the road.

It's a small scenic pull-off, there's a twenty-foot trail—now blanketed with deep, undisturbed snow—that leads under fanning tree branches to a view of the mountain dipping lazily down toward Romeo.

The mountains here in Upstate are not the towering sharply pointed behemoths of the west, nor are they the majestic blue and purple-tinged rolling mountains of the south, no, the mountains here are gentle, timeworn—they look like a fluffy down comforter thrown over a bed and not smoothed out. The low waves and ripples are our mountains. I prefer them above all others.

"This is a new Christmas tradition?" Gabe asks, his presence warming the car faster than any heater could.

"I hope so." I turn off the car, the engine cutting out and leaving only the winter silence of outside and the puff of our breath still hanging in the cold air. "Come on."

I hop out of the car, the winter biting at my cheeks and filling my lungs. It's late afternoon, and the sun is falling, sliding down the mountain. It gets dark early in winter this far north, the sky is already deep gray blue fading toward purple.

The snow sinks beneath my feet and when I shut my door it echoes over the woods.

While Gabe climbs out of his side I walk to the back of the car and open the trunk. It creaks, the canary yellow paint flashing against the snowy woods like the feathers of a flying wood thrush. The scent of gasoline drifts up from the darkness.

"I was hoping this wouldn't be a tradition..." Gabe says, walking around the car, brushing his fingers over my cheek, playing with the hair coming out from under my winter hat.

I scoff and then lean toward him, his warmth pulling me in.

The road is deserted, the mountainside quiet. The winter wind and the smell of snow are our only companions. With my family at the cabin, I won't find a quieter place to do this.

Plus Miss Erma said I *knew* what to do.

Which means, well, it means what I knew and should've acknowledged the second I laid eyes on Gabe stalking toward me in his office in New York.

I didn't realize though that I'd be so scared of this moment. I always thought that when I found the man I believed was my soul mate that I'd give him this gift at the first opportunity. I always imagined that it'd be like my parents—both Christmas lovers—and I'd know without a doubt that this was the right thing to do.

It's funny how I never thought to give this gift to Jason, which means that I knew, even if I wasn't ready to admit it, that he wasn't the one.

And now, here I am, after only two days of knowing Gabe, ready to give him my heart.

I reach into the depths of the dark trunk, the black carpet swallowing the fading light. The space is empty except for one thing—my present.

I grip it and pull it out. The present is a little larger than a book, but lighter. The paper is metallic red, crisply folded, and wrapped with a large gold bow. The wrapping paper has a few scuff marks, it's years old after all, and the bow is creased and flattened from bumping around the trunk.

As I squeeze the cold present in my hands, the icy air catches in my lungs. I've been carrying this present around with me for so many years it's frightening to finally let it go.

"Do you want to see the overlook?" I ask, shutting the trunk carefully.

"Alright," Gabe says, pulling his warm fingers from the back of my neck where he'd been playing with my hair.

We're bundled in all the winter gear the cabin had to offer—hats, down-filled jackets, knitted scarves—but it's still nose-nippingly cold.

Gabe leads the way, and I follow behind, stepping in his deep footprints, hanging on to his hand, holding the present in my other.

The trees arch overhead, shading the light and creating a snow tunnel that leads to the vista's edge. The trees part at the end of the trail, breaking open at a rustic wooden fence piled high with snow.

From the wooden fence, the mountain slopes gently down, rolling over snow-bathed stones and evergreens, until miles beyond, there's Romeo, cradled in the valley, next to the river, lit up like a watercolor village on a Christmas card.

With dusk arriving, the Christmas lights of Romeo glow brightly and if they made sound, they'd sound like chiming bells and choral voices.

"Isn't it magical?" I ask, staring out over the valley.

When Gabe doesn't answer, I glance at him, only to find that he isn't looking at Romeo, he's watching me with a small smile.

Warmth flows over me like I just took a long sip of steaming hot cocoa and I feel my cheeks flushing. When Gabe sees this, his smile grows wider.

I hold the present out to him, the golden setting sun catching the metallic red of the paper. The cold wind strums the bow, thrumming it quietly.

"What is it?" Gabe asks, his brow lowering. He looks from the present back to me, frowning. "It was in the trunk with me."

I nod, my hands shaking. "It's a Christmas present. For you."

Gabe closes his hands over mine. His are warm, strong, and when he wraps my hands in his I stop shaking.

"Why are you nervous?" He studies me in the quickly fading light.

"I'm not," I say hurriedly, and Gabe smiles at me, lifting an eyebrow. Apparently he can read my prevarication as well as I can read his.

He takes the present then, holding the careworn package in his hands.

"I haven't opened a Christmas present in nearly twenty years," he says, then he looks back to me quickly, as if he didn't realize he'd said that out loud and he's afraid he's said too much.

My chest tightens. Nearly twenty years means that he was just a boy when he stopped receiving gifts.

By the look on his face he doesn't want my pity, so I merely say, "Well, that means now is an especially good time to open one."

He shakes it, almost like a little kid trying to figure out what's inside.

"You had this before you met me though," he says, studying the package, his fingers running over the smooth paper.

In the valley below, more lights wink on, brightening the falling darkness. I nod and step closer to Gabe, wanting to bury myself against him to soak in all his warmth and the delicious winter smell of him.

"I wrapped it years ago, after I talked to Miss Erma about my soul mate."

He stills then and searches my expression. "She told you to give your soul mate this gift?"

I nod, my heart thundering in my ears.

"You think I'm your soul mate?"

There's a yearning in his eyes, a longing. I nod again.

"Why? I don't love Christmas. Wasn't that a requirement?" The look on his face begs me to contradict him.

I shake my head, the wool yarn of the scarf tickling my chin. "She said that when I met my soul mate I'd know. And then, when I knew, I was supposed to give him this gift. That he'd know what it meant."

The way he looks at the gift is part fear, part fervent hope. "What if I don't know what it means? What if it's not for me?"

"It is," I say, scared but certain.

"How do you know?"

"Because I love you," I whisper, reaching out, putting my hand on top of his, "Because every day with you feels like Christmas. If it's not for you, I don't care. I want every day with you."

Gabe studies me for a quiet moment. All the world around us silent.

"Can I put this down?" he finally asks, gesturing at the present.

My lips wobble and I press them flat.

He doesn't want it?

I nod sharply, my throat closing. Gabe bends down, sets it gently in the snow drift. It glistens red against the white. I stare at it forlornly. He doesn't want it. He doesn't want my love.

But when he looks back to me, his eyes are lit with need. I pull in a sharp breath.

"Say that part again," he growls, taking a step forward through the deep snow.

"Every day feels like Christmas with you?" I bite my bottom lip at the heated look in his eyes.

"Not that part." He takes another step forward and my heart quickens.

"I want every day with you?"

He takes another step forward, lines his body against mine, looks down at me. "Not that part."

I reach up and grip the warmth of his jacket. He tugs me close, pressing the length of him against me. I tilt my face up, my lips part, and I can already taste him on me.

"You mean, when I said I love you?" I ask, my veins full of toasty, fiery warmth.

He smiles then. A beautiful, winter's eve, stockings-over-the-fireplace, joyful smile. "I love you too."

Then there isn't any more talking, because he captures my mouth with his and presses me down into the soft, waiting snowbank.

35

GABE

I don't feel the cold. I don't see the dark. It's all rushing heat and bright shining light.

I hold Natalie, stroke my hands over her cheeks, draw whispered sounds from her to greedily drink down.

She said the view is magical, but she's the one with magic. I've been closed off for years, limping through life, and the second I met her she turned on all the lights and pulled me forward, back into life. Even without the soul mate present, I know. Even without someone else telling me, I know.

Natalie is the woman I want to spend every Christmas with, from here on out.

The wind rushes over my back, blowing a cloud of snow past, chilling my cheeks. I cover Natalie, tucking her beneath me to shield her from the chill.

She sends her hands into my coat, under my shirt, and then presses her cold hands to my hips. She bites my lip at the same time and my blood flames as her hands search lower, unbuttoning my jeans.

I taste her, lick her sugary sweet icing and cookie flavor, and then trail my mouth down her cheek and over her jaw. The wind gusts again, snowflakes swirl around us. I'm nearly mindless with the desire to be inside her. She grips me in her hands and I jerk in her tight hold.

"I love you," she whispers against my mouth, her hand stroking down my length.

With that, I whip off my coat, lay it on the snow as a bed for her, warmed from my body heat. The cold pricks at my bare arms. I don't care.

Natalie grins up at me, mischievous as mistletoe, and grips me tight as she leans close and wraps her mouth over me.

I strain to hold still. I pray that I can be as quiet and still as the forest around us. But I can't. A low growling noise rumbles from me and I jerk beneath her mouth and tongue.

I take her hair in my hand, hold her close as she swirls her tongue over me like she's licking the icing off a sugar cookie.

"Natalie," I say, straining to hold still beneath her hot candy cane-red mouth. "Let me—"

She reaches to the side then, grabs a handful of freshly fallen, fluffy snow, and pulls her mouth from me. The heat, the wetness of her leaving me is hit with the cold of the night. Then she pops the snow in her mouth, lets it melt on her tongue, and takes me again.

Cold and heat. Fire and Ice. Her mouth is so cold it

feels hot, so hot it feels cold. She hums around me and I can't...I can't take any more.

"Let me—" I say again, and when she pulls her mouth from me, I push her back onto my coat and yank her jeans down to her ankles. "Let me love you," I finish, thrusting inside her.

The heat of her, the desperate heat, it's everything. She presses her icy cold mouth to mine, I thrust my tongue into her mouth, I thrust into her. I'm consumed. I'm warmed to my soul. Her heat reaches my heart.

She cries out, and as I stroke her and bury my heart deep inside her, I feel her wrap around me, hold me tight. She comes undone, and I follow.

I'll always follow her.

Natalie lies in my arms, nestled in the soft downy snowbank.

We're wrapped up again in our clothes and coats and scarves, a barrier against the evening chill and our bed of snow.

The sky is inky black and the stars wink overhead like snowflakes in heaven. Beneath us, the snow looks as if we decided to make a dozen snow angels, one over the other.

I take a deep breath of the frosty, evergreen air and turn my lips to Natalie, brushing them over the soft skin of her jaw. Her lips tilt up in a smile and I press a kiss to the corner of her mouth.

She's staring at the sky, watching the beginnings of an evening snowfall, fat lazy flakes drifting down.

"Merry Christmas," she says, turning to me, a happy smile lighting her face.

I press another kiss to her. "Should I say 'bah humbug'?"

She laughs, her shoulders shaking as I pull her closer.

"You want me to open the present?" I ask, glancing over at the package still resting in the snowbank.

"It's yours," Natalie says with confidence, "I've been keeping it for you for years."

"And if it isn't?" I ask, although I can't fathom that it wouldn't be. There isn't any way that I'm not meant to spend my life with her.

"First of all, it is. Second, if for some reason it isn't, I'll just tie you up with Christmas lights, park you under the mistletoe and have my way with you."

"For how long?" I ask. I'm not exactly opposed to this idea.

She grins at me. "For as long as it takes for you to admit you're mine."

I scoff. "I've already admitted that."

She sits up, leaving cold air where her warmth was, the snow crunching beneath her.

"Good. Then you can open it and we'll have done our part in making another Romeo soul mate Christmas story come true."

She stands to grab the present, then brings it back to me. And even if she says she isn't nervous and doesn't care, there's still a hopeful tension in the bend of her shoulders and the half-smile on her lips.

I nod and take the present, tracing the crisply taped edges of the package.

"How long have you been carrying this around?"

"Ten years." She shrugs, sitting down next to me, sinking into the snow.

The wind whistles past, swirling snowflakes around us. Natalie pulls her scarf tighter around her neck and leans close as I slowly unravel the gold bow.

"Long time to wait," I say, dropping the bow into her hands. She clasps the ribbon, her hand folding around it.

"It was worth it," she says, her voice as hushed as the snowy woods.

My heart beats loud, painfully, as I tear the edge of the paper, pull back the red wrapping to reveal the white cardboard box. I crumple the wrapping paper and put it in my pocket. Natalie's eyes nearly glow as she stares at the box in my hands.

She's certain that I'm going to know what this gift means. I'm terrified that I won't.

I lift the lid, revealing old, crinkled red tissue paper. I push it aside, the fragile paper rustling. A snowflake falls on the paper, and then another.

I stare at the gift for Natalie's soul mate.

Ten years she's had this.

Ten years.

The wind rushes in my ears, the cold stings my skin and seeps to my bones, the night blinds me.

"Well?" Natalie asks, her voice far away.

I shake my head, my throat tightening on the words.
I was afraid I wouldn't know what the gift meant.
I was afraid I wouldn't recognize it.
But how could I not?
How couldn't I recognize Lee?

36

GABE

I lift the gold heart Christmas ornament from the tissue paper.

It's smaller than I remember, only about the size of a ripe plum. The cold of the metal stings and the sharp point at the end of the heart digs into my palm.

I loosen my grip, hold it gently. It's as light as a snowflake, the gold-plated metal is as smooth as ice, and the color is still that burnished golden star shade.

There are midnight blue crystals embedded in the gold—fifteen of them, I know. The navy blue ribbon is still soft, its edges frayed, the bow tied at the top.

I rub the ribbon between my thumb and forefinger, remembering when I clumsily tied the bow, tugging it tight.

I know what I'll find, my breath is short, my chest tight, but still I flip the ornament over. Even in the dark, with the cold frosting the gold, I can make out exactly what I knew I'd find.

I run my thumb over the engraving—First Christmas, LC.

Lee Cavanaugh.

"Where did you get this?" I ask, my head bowed.

There's an image in my mind, the one I've tried to bury under mountains of snow. The crooked Christmas tree, popcorn strung on thread, baking gingerbread, "Deck the Halls" banged out on an out-of-tune piano, and Lee holding this ornament.

I turn to Natalie and push the words out, past the storm of images in my mind and the clamoring of my heart fighting to be heard, because...Lee.

"Where did you get this," I demand, my voice ragged, my hand shaking.

I realize then that I must look frightening because Natalie's staring at me like she's never seen me before.

I know my face feels like a tight mask, holding back all the emotions galloping around my chest. My shoulders are stiff, my chest aching, the wind rushing around me echoing the howl inside that I never let out.

"I..." Natalie frowns at me, reaches out and touches the back of my hand, brushing her fingers over me. "At the Romeo Christmas fair ten years ago. Are you alright?"

"Yes."

No. No, I'm not alright.

I close my eyes, block out the sight of Natalie's pink cheeks, her hair curling out from underneath her red knitted winter hat and the snowflakes lighting in her hair and melting on her cheeks. I can still smell her though, that gingerbread and icing scent. I can feel her too, the warmth of her and the current that sparks between us as bright as the North Star.

Natalie moves closer, the snow scuffing beneath her. She leans against me, resting her head on my arm. Slowly the tension rolling through me unravels, and all the questions I have coalesce into the only one that matters.

"Tell me exactly what happened. Who you bought it from. What they looked like. Where they were. When. Every detail you remember."

Natalie stiffens against me. I can feel the weight of her gaze studying me. I shake my head. "Tell me."

"You recognize it then? It means something?"

I give a sharp nod.

She pulls me closer then, wrapping her arms through mine, her breath warm on my neck as she leans into me.

The snowbank is cold now that dark is fully here, the cold seeps through my jeans, the snow caking onto the fabric and biting at my skin.

The trees surrounding us rustle in the wind, heaving a quiet sigh as the weight of the snow shifts on their branches. In the valley below, Romeo blazes bright with Christmas lights reflecting off the snow.

I turn to Natalie, focus on the green of her eyes, shaded to gray in the dark of the night.

"Natalie..." I say, my voice breaking.

"Okay," she begins, her breath a light mist in front of her. "Ten years ago, I asked Miss Erma about my soul mate."

"Right." I nod and squeeze the heart ornament in my hand.

"She said everything I've already told you. We were at the annual Christmas fair, where there are booths with crafts, decorations, gifts, cookies and hot drinks. I'd bought this ornament already and Miss Erma saw it in my hand and she said, that is for your soul mate. Give it to him as a Christmas gift, he'll know what it means." She pauses, then asks, "Do you?"

"Yes." I reach over when Natalie shivers and wrap an arm around her. "Tell me about who you bought it from."

She bites her bottom lip, her brow furrowing as she looks out over the lights of Romeo down in the valley below.

"He wasn't from Romeo. I'd never seen him before. Nobody knew him." She shakes her head, "He hasn't been back since that year."

My chest tightens. "What did he look like?"

The snow falls around us, picking up speed, filling the sky with white as Natalie thinks it over.

"I can't remember much. He was younger than me, maybe fifteen? He was selling wooden ornaments, this was the only metal ornament. I bought it because he told me that this ornament was full of Christmas magic. I asked him why he wasn't keeping it then and he told me he'd used up all his Christmas magic already."

If I'd had any doubts, they just vanished. Lee and I always said that this ornament was full of magic, no one else would know that.

"Can you remember," I ask, "the color of his eyes? His hair? If he seemed healthy? Happy? Was he with anyone else?"

Natalie shakes her head. "He was alone. He seemed happy. He...maybe...he looked..." Natalie searches my features, takes in my jaw, my sharp nose, my dark brown eyes, my black hair, her eyes widen and she says, "He looked like you."

The last of the ice around my heart cracks and falls to the ground like icicles shattering in spring.

I always thought that Natalie was like the ghost of Christmas Present, showing me all the ways the Christmas of now could be wonderful—family, togetherness, giving.

She was also the ghost of Christmas Future, giving me a glimpse of the joy of years to come. I never thought that she was also the ghost of Christmas Past.

Yet here she is, reaching into my chest, pulling out my heart, and showing me that there still is Christmas magic in the world.

It's then that she reaches up, her cold hand brushing over my cheek. "You're crying."

I shake my head. "I gave up. We thought he was gone."

"Who?" Her fingers brush my cheeks, as gentle as a kiss.

"Lee. My brother. This was his." I hold up the

ornament and it catches the light of the moon, glinting softly. It's warm now, the metal has soaked up the heat of my hand.

"Why did you think he was gone?"

I let out a shuddering breath, remembering the last Christmas I ever celebrated.

"When I was seven we went to Rockefeller Center for the tree lighting. Lee was four. He and I were inseparable, we did everything together, my mom always said we were stuck together like two sides of a coin. He had this ornament, it was his from his first Christmas and he took it everywhere with him."

I heft the ornament, still not quite believing that it's here, which means Lee is still here.

"Rockefeller Center was packed, imagine Times Square on New Year's, and then make yourself a child surrounded by noise and people jostling and jarring you." I tighten my jaw, hating to think about it. "Lee and I were holding hands, my mom always had us hold hands in busy areas, so we wouldn't get separated. My mom said, don't lose your brother, Gabe." My mouth twists. "Then the lights of the tree turned on, the Christmas carols started, and I forgot about Lee. All I could think about was how big the tree was, how bright the lights were, and how many presents would be under our tree at home. I was enthralled by the carolers. "Have Yourself a Merry Little Christmas" is what they were singing. I was swept away by all that Christmas, the sparkling ornaments, the glow of the lights, the peppermint taste of candy canes, the idea that in no time at all Santa would be bringing presents and Lee and I would run to the living room and...that's when I remembered Lee and realized he wasn't holding my hand anymore. He wasn't holding my mom's hand either. Or my dad's."

"He was lost?"

I shake my head. "Lost. Taken. I don't know. We never found him. He was just gone. I thought he'd be back. I thought he'd be found. If not the next day, then the day after that, then I thought he'd be there for Christmas. But Christmas Day, when I woke up and ran to the living room, Lee wasn't there. Neither was the tree or any presents or any decorations. My parents had taken them down. They never mentioned Christmas again. After years of desperation, they stopped mentioning Lee too. Just like they took down the tree and the decorations, they took down all the pictures of my brother. The reminder of him was too painful so they wiped him away. If they could have they would've wiped me away too. I was the one who lost him. If I hadn't been so engrossed with the Christmas tree—"

"You were seven," Natalie says. "You were a child. You aren't to blame."

I smile at the blazing light in her eyes, defending my childhood self. "I still let him go. Child or not. If I hadn't, he'd still be here."

"But he is here," she says, covering my hand with her own, capturing the heart ornament between us. "Isn't that what this means? He's still here."

"I gave up looking," I say, swallowing down the shame. "When I was eighteen I started working night jobs while I went to school, and everything I made I sent to private investigators. But I had nothing for them to go on and they never found anything. When I turned twenty-five I gave up. Both my parents had died, convinced Lee was gone. I convinced myself he was gone too."

"But he's not," she says. "At least, ten years ago he wasn't."

I smile at Natalie. "I hated Christmas for taking my brother. But now, it's given me you and it's—"

"Given you back your brother."

I nod. "He's out there. Maybe he doesn't remember me. I don't know what happened. But I'm going to start looking again. This time, I won't give up."

Natalie clasps my hand. "I'll help you, if you'd like."

I brush my mouth over hers. "Thank you."

For years Christmas was a reminder of everything I'd lost, but now it's a beacon leading me back to everything I love.

37

GABE

DECEMBER 24, 1:43 AM

I CAN'T SLEEP.

Natalie curls next to me, her hand warm on my chest, her breathing soft and even.

She kicked back the feather comforter in her sleep. It pools around our feet, and the heat from the vent overhead blows over us. The dark of the bedroom plays with moonlight glistening off snow and frost.

I've been watching the shadows flicker on the walls for hours, my mind conjuring pasts and futures and what ifs.

After we drove back to the cabin, Natalie answered all my questions, and then she answered them again and again. Then she got our phones (of course) and she called someone named Wanda, the organizer of the

Christmas Fair to see if she had any information—she didn't.

I called the investigator in charge of my brother's case, and the private investigator I'd worked with in the past, giving them the scant information I had. It's not much to go on, but it's more than we've had in the past.

Wanda promised Natalie that she'd look through her records and see if she could find Lee's booth registration form and Natalie promised to ask around Romeo. She swore someone would know something.

Natalie even called Erma, the woman who predicted that someday Natalie and I would meet, but she didn't know anything beyond the fact that ten years ago, when she spotted that ornament, she'd seen Natalie and me together.

But after the flurry of calls there was nothing to do except have dinner with Natalie's family, do the dishes, play a round of Scrabble with Grandma Agnes and then go to bed.

I've been here before. Not with Natalie curled against me, that's not what I mean. I've been here in this hope-filled crevice that keeps you awake at night and so on edge that you expect a phone call any moment. The phone call never comes but your body doesn't know that. It stays adrenaline filled, muscles tight, mind expectant.

Which is why I am still wide awake in the middle of the night, on Christmas Eve, expecting (but not really expecting) Lee to appear for Christmas.

I let out a long sigh, stretching over the sheets, finding the cool spot at the edge of the bed.

Natalie makes a noise in her sleep and turns over, pulling the sheets with her. I smile at the shadows and light playing over her.

She's mine. I love her. I knew it the minute I first saw her, but I was fooled into doubting it by the mistletoe and the gingerbread. I don't doubt it anymore.

I carefully slip out of bed, the sheets rustling and the mattress groaning, and step into my borrowed jeans and T-shirt. By the fluorescent blue numbers on the alarm clock, it's nearly two in the morning. The middle of the night is as good of a time as any to do what I should've done years ago. I'm going to set things right.

When Natalie first met me she said I was a scrooge. She was right. I was.

Christmas is coming. It's Christmas Eve and I only have a day to do what I need. On the nightstand, the silver of Natalie's car keys glints in the moonlight. She isn't hiding the keys anymore, she doesn't think she needs to.

But I have to get back to the city. I brush a kiss across her lips, careful not to wake her, and slip from the bedroom.

38

NATALIE

GABE IS GONE.

When I woke up to the morning light falling through the window, his side of the bed was empty and cold, the indentation from his weight long gone. I wasn't concerned. Not at first.

The smells coming from the kitchen were of coffee and bacon and waffles. There was the clanking of dishes being set on the table, the indistinguishable conversation of my mom and grandma prodding Felix to find a date for New Year's.

I stretched my legs, wiggled my toes, smiled at the frosted window and the wooden black bear lamp on the nightstand. I was feeling cozy, toasty, sleep-kissed, remembering the way Gabe and I made love before I drifted off.

I dressed in a hurry, came out to the living room to find Gabe, and then...didn't.

He was gone.

My car was gone.

"When do you think Gabe will be back?" my mom asks, pouring maple syrup over her Belgian waffle.

She's in her Christmas Eve dress, a long denim dress with snowflakes for buttons, which she has worn every Christmas Eve since I was a kid. We're around the breakfast table and we're all wearing our Christmas Eve outfits—a tradition.

I'm in my red velvet dress and flashing bulb jewelry, which is the only fancy outfit I have here.

My brother is in his ugly sweater, an olive green and brick red monstrosity with the abominable snowman shaking a present, that he has worn since he was a teen.

My dad has on his red corduroy Christmas vest and hunter green corduroy pants, which my mom made for him and he swears fit as well as they did twenty-five years ago.

My grandma changes things up every year. This year she's in a sequined silver pantsuit which she says is supposed to be an icicle.

My dad puts down his coffee mug and studies me. He frowns. "Where did you say he was going?"

I didn't say. I didn't say where he went. I didn't say when he'd be back. I didn't say anything except not to hold breakfast for him.

Because frankly, I don't know where he went and I don't know if he'll be back.

The sausage, which I'm sure is delicious, tastes like dried mud and ash as I try to swallow. I take a long gulp of my steaming black coffee to help it down. The bitter brew burns my throat.

Felix watches me with sharp eyes while he reaches for another waffle. "Did he escape? Is this part of his acting thing? Are we supposed to go catch him?"

"Ooooh fun," Grandma Agnes says, then she smacks Felix's hand and grabs the waffle he was going to take. "Age before beauty."

Felix gives Grandma a charming smile. "Aww thanks, Grandma."

"Don't thanks Grandma me. I see all the girls twittering after you. You can thank your Grandpa Heath, he was a handsome devil. Knew when to settle down too. In my day, men knew how to be men. They met a woman and asked her to marry him within a day. One day! True love! Now that's how it's done. I was a female war bride, met my husband in France—"

"Oh brother," my dad says, taking a bite of bacon and shaking his head. He usually doesn't mind my grandma's stories unless it's before he's had his coffee.

My mom pats my dad's hand, then says, "Mother. That was a Cary Grant movie about World War II! You and Dad met in 1968 and dated for a year—"

"Some people claim that, but others say we were in France and"—Grandma turns to me and narrows her eyes—"speaking of Cary Grant, when is your actor coming back?"

"Soon," I say, nodding emphatically. With my family, if you nod while you say something, they inevitably believe you.

Well, all except Felix, who learned as a kid to use the same exact trick. He narrows his eyes on me and scratches his chin. "I thought I heard him leave around two."

"In the morning?" my mom says, her eyebrows raising nearly to her hairline. "Did you fight?" she asks, turning to me.

I shake my head. "No. It's fine. He'll be back."

I take another bite of the sausage, forcing myself to chew and smile.

"We're not supposed to chase him?" Grandma asks, a hopeful glint in her eyes. "I'd love that. Is he hiding out in Romeo?"

"No." I wish.

But if what Felix says is true, then Gabe made love to me, waited for me to fall asleep, then took my keys, snuck out of the house, and left.

He went back to New York. Exactly where he's been trying to get back to ever since I took him away.

The sausage hits my stomach, and a twisty nausea overwhelms me. He never stopped trying to leave, I just stopped trying to make him stay.

Until Felix said that Gabe left in the middle of the night, I had a flickering hope that he'd only left an hour ago to pick up a gift, or groceries, or...I don't know.

But now? If he left at two in the morning, that means even if we're soul mates, even if we're meant to be, it doesn't mean that we'll end up together.

And maybe it's selfish of me to want him here. He has his brother to find. He has...families to evict. He has a life. Maybe...maybe he was just playing along, doing what he had to do to get back to New York.

I look down at my hand and realize that I'm clutching my fork so tightly my knuckles have turned white. I loosen my hand and set my fork onto my plate.

He fooled me. He left me.

Yet, I can't believe that of Gabe. I won't.

"He'll be back," I say again, more firmly.

"Good," my dad says, "as long as he's here in time for the Christmas cake. He won't want to miss his chance at finding the star."

There's a knock at the front door, loud and firm. I jump and scoot my chair back from the table. It's him. He's back.

Relief rushes over me, filling me with Christmas joy. Of course he's back. He wouldn't leave, not after yesterday, not after promising me all the Christmases for the rest of our lives.

"He's back," I say, pushing my chair in. "I'll get it."

The knock sounds again and I hurry to the front door and swing it wide, a happy smile on my face. "I was worried. Where'd you—"

It's not Gabe.

The cold winter air hits me and I freeze.

"Sorry about this, Natalie," Luke Travinci, Romeo's favorite police officer says, "but I'm going to need you to come down to the station."

My grandma pushes past me. "For what? It's Christmas Eve!" Then she smiles at Luke as he takes off his hat and nods to her politely.

"Ma'am."

"Come on in for waffles," Grandma says. "Tell us about it inside."

She likes Luke. She and his grandpa went to the junior prom together. Luke is five years older than me, tall and lanky like a cowboy. Last time I visited home he let me off with a warning instead of giving me a speeding ticket. Usually he has a soft spot for me.

But by the tightness around his mouth I can tell that soft spot isn't going to do me any good today.

"Well?" Grandma asks.

Luke shakes his head. My family has gathered behind me and my grandma so they hear it when he says, "Natalie has to come in. She's wanted for questioning regarding the disappearance of Gabriel Cavanaugh."

There's a stunned silence.

"Dang! You mean she really did kidnap him?" Grandma says in a loud, shocked voice.

At that, Luke takes us all down to the station.

39

GABE

"You're alive!" Cecily slams into me, throwing her arms around me and burying her head into my chest.

She's short, five one with shoes on, but she packs a punch when she wants to. Right now, she wants to, because she backs up and slams her fist into my chest.

"Cec—" I hold up my hands.

"That's for making me worry!" She punches me again. "And that's for not calling! And that's for disappearing! And that's—"

I grab her wrist and tug her in for another hug. I grin down at my red-faced cousin. "Thanks for worrying about me."

I pull her close. She's in her puffy winter coat, Christmasaurus pajama pants and fuzzy house slippers.

I'm guessing that when she got my text this morning she immediately hopped out of bed and into a taxi so that she could accost me in person.

I'm at my office in Midtown. The lights are dim, the air cool and dry, the smell of the whisky shattered over the floor is gone, cleaned in my absence, and replaced with the scent of industrial cleaner.

The space I once considered a haven from Christmas madness now feels sterile, barren, and cold.

Outside my office door the rows of desks stand empty. From the windows, a light snow falls to the city street, the white specks painted against the crowded buildings and the blue-gray early morning sky.

No one is at the office today. I sent out a company-wide memo that Christmas Eve through Boxing Day were paid holidays and so far no one has shown.

Except my cousin.

Cecily sniffs, the cold from outside still clinging to her jacket and her cheeks. She pushes back from me and puts her hands on her hips, which means she's in mad mom mode. She gets the same exact look when she's yelling at Jeb for coloring on the walls or when she's scolding June for refusing to eat her green beans.

"Of course I worried. You went missing! Your assistant said you were taking the week off, which I knew was a load of crap. Then you didn't answer your phone or your door. After twenty-four hours of silence I contacted the police—"

"You what?"

"—and they found the video footage of you getting in that woman's car. The one you had security bar from the building. The police picked her up—"

"They what?"

"—and she better have a good lawyer because..." Cecily pauses. Looks at my expression. Her red-faced indignation is there one second, and then it's gone, like a Christmas tree unplugged.

She points her finger at me. "You like her."

Cecily always has been able to read me well.

It's hard not to smile. "I love her."

"Love?" Cecily makes a choking sound and then hits her chest with her fist. I grab the coffee off my desk and offer her the mug. She waves it off. "I'm fine. Just surprised. What's her name?"

"Natalie Fiorre." I grin. "She's a professional decorator. Loves Christmas. Lives in the Hudson Apartments." I gesture at the pile of papers on my desk and the open windows on my computer screen. "I've been working all night. We're not going to tear it down, we're going to renovate it."

It's what I should've done in the first place, I see it now. Natalie is right, it's more than a building. It's a community.

"She convinced you to renovate instead of evict? I like her already."

"There's more," I say, leaning forward. "She met Lee. She saw him ten years ago. He's..."

Cecily's hands clench and her face fills with color. "He's alive."

I nod. "He's alive. I don't know where he is, but ten years ago he was in Romeo—"

"We'll find him," Cecily says.

We will. I know he's out there. That ornament, Lee

may have thought it was all out of Christmas magic, but it wasn't. It brought me Natalie, and it brought me news of him. It has at least one more bit of magic left, because we're going to find him.

Cecily hugs me again, a quick, fierce hug, because of anyone alive, she knows what this means. When she pulls back she gives me an apologetic smile.

"Just so you know, I'm fairly certain your Natalie was hauled into the station this morning. Handcuffs. Back of the police car. Prison bars. You know."

I do know. It's exactly what I told Natalie would happen that first night we were together. Except I didn't actually think it would happen.

I shake my head and grab my wool coat from my desk chair. It's been eight hours since I left Romeo. Everything took longer than I expected. The drive, showering and changing at home, halting the Hudson Apartments eviction process, buying a ring.

I shrug my coat on and wrap the red cashmere scarf around my neck. I'll leave Natalie's car in my apartment garage. Taking my SUV will be faster on the snowy roads.

"I'm heading out," I tell Cecily, flicking off the lights and striding toward the elevator.

"Where are you going?" Cecily says, keeping pace.

I hit the elevator button and smile at her. "To bail the woman I'm going to marry out of jail. Maybe you could make a call and let them know I'm on my way?"

The elevator doors slide open, spilling light across the dim office.

"Marry!" Cecily hurries onto the elevator.

"If she'll have me."

Cecily's brow furrows, and despite her dinosaur Christmas pajama bottoms, she manages to look fierce when she says, "You're bringing her to Christmas dinner. The both of you are coming. No maybes. No pretend thinking about it. No—"

"Wouldn't miss it," I say as the doors slide open.

I leave a stunned Cecily in the lobby of the building as I hurry onto the snowy sidewalk.

Natalie's in jail.

She probably thinks I left her.

There isn't a chance of that happening. Now I just need to make it back in time for Christmas.

40

THE POLICE STATION IS ATTACHED TO CITY HALL, A beautiful three-story stone building in downtown Romeo, built in the mid-eighteen hundreds.

It was constructed from rough-hewn beige sandstone and has a large clock tower and bright shiny windows looking over Main Street. The whole building is wrapped in a red bow, so that it looks like a present and there are snowflake lights hanging from all the windows.

Outside, snow piles on the sidewalks and frosts the stone so it looks like gingerbread dipped in frosting. Inside, the small corner of City Hall that belongs to the police station is decorated with garland, colored lights, and a large poinsettia on the administrative desk.

It looks like Luke's fellow officer Mia decorated. It's an annual battle between the two of them. One that she always wins. There's also a plastic tub full of freshly baked Christmas cookies, mixing the scent of cinnamon with the bitter smell of drip coffee.

Luke is one of two officers in Romeo, and today he's the only one on duty. We're sitting at a round fake wood table in the small break room. There's a tiny kitchenette, the table, and four folding chairs.

There aren't many other options though. I've not been here really except for our field trip back in elementary, but it hasn't changed much. The station has the admin area, Luke's office, Mia's office, the space where fingerprinting and background checks are run, a storage area, and a holding area.

Last time I came, when I was eight, I got a sticker. I don't think I'm getting a sticker this time.

My family left after giving their statements. My mom shot me worried glances the whole time, my dad was solemn, my grandma told stories about women in her day, and Felix asked Luke if he was going to play hockey this weekend. When they were gone Luke sat me in the break room and poured me a cup of coffee.

We've been here for two hours and counting. The coffee is cold, my back hurts from sitting in the cheap chair for so long, and the break room clock ticks the seconds down.

I've already answered Luke's questions. I don't know where Gabe is. I don't know if he's coming back. He took my car and left. I didn't "disappear" him. It's all a misunderstanding. End of story.

"Are you going to let me go soon?" I ask, shoving my coffee mug across the faux wood. "If you don't I'm going to send you out for SweetStop coffee. This stuff tastes like you used a dirty sock as a filter."

Luke puts on his stern cop look and crosses his arms over his chest. His uniform stretches across his shoulders and his jaw goes hard. The intimidation tactic might work if I didn't remember when he was four feet tall and playing with toy cars.

"Come on, it's Christmas Eve. My mom's cooking dinner as we speak. You wouldn't want me to miss it."

Luke sighs and rubs his hand down his jaw. "That's exactly it," he says, scraping his chair legs back over the linoleum tiles. "My mom invited an old friend's daughter over for dinner. Christmas Eve set-up. If you leave then I have no excuse to miss it."

I lift an eyebrow. Luke's mom must be getting desperate for grandchildren. I shrug.

"Just tell your mom no."

He gives me a hard look.

His mom is a former Army drill sergeant, there isn't really telling her no if she wants something bad enough.

"You really don't want to go?" I ask, taking another swallow of the terrible station coffee.

He shakes his head no. A definite no.

"Fine." I lean back and the chair squeaks. "I'll stay."

His shoulders relax.

"But I'm free to go if I want to?"

He nods. Then asks, "You really brought him here because of Miss Erma?" He shakes his head like he can't quite believe it.

"What? You've lived here all your life. You know as well as I do that you don't ignore Miss Erma."

He mutters something under his breath and grips his coffee mug. "I swear trouble follows that woman. The explosion at the dig site. The injury on the mountain bike trail. The missing person fiasco with all that dang media coverage. Now you, 'scrooging' a man."

"None of that has to do with Miss Erma," I say, indignant on her behalf.

"It all has to do with her. Every bit of trouble."

Luke's brown eyes are hard and his grip on his cup is even harder, which makes me wonder...

"Are you scared Miss Erma is going to see your soul mate or scared she won't?"

Luke lifts his eyebrows. "Let's just say I'd rather shoot off my own finger than be saddled with a soul mate prediction."

"Which finger?"

"Any of them."

I pat Luke's hand. "Good luck with that."

Before he can answer, his work cell rings. "Travinci."

He listens to the person on the other end, his eyes narrowing on me. The old coffee tastes bitter in my mouth and my stomach does a slide.

I hear the name Cavanaugh, something indistinguishable. Luke makes confirmation noises, says his thanks, and then hangs up. He puts his phone on the table and lets out a long-suffering sigh.

"Well?" I ask, my mouth dry. When I see my hand shaking I grip my mug tightly to make it stop.

By Luke's expression I'm imagining the worst. Gabe was in an accident. He's still missing. Or...he's pressing charges?

Luke shakes his head. "Gabe Cavanaugh is back in New York. His cousin called it in when she found him working. He confirmed it."

Gabe's back at his office?

I picture it. The depressing gray walls, the lack of Christmas cheer, the paper shredder shredding dreams, and Gabe sitting at his desk, all alone. What is he doing? What is he thinking?

Is he going through with the evictions?

No. He wouldn't.

I stand, thrusting my chair back, the legs scraping across the linoleum tile.

"Where are you going?" Luke asks, standing too.

"New York." There's only one person I want to spend Christmas with, and if he isn't here then I'm going to him.

Luke levels me with his flat-eyed intimidation stare. "You're throwing me to the wolves? If you stay we could play an eight-hour game of Risk."

"Sorry." I pat his arm. "Have fun on your blind date. But I have to go after him." I frown at Luke, eye the handcuffs on his belt and then say, "Can I borrow—"

"No."

"I wouldn't necessarily use—"

"No."

"What about—"

"No."

"Whatever, I'll just use the Christmas lights again."

Luke points at the break room door. "Get out of here. Go find your soul mate. Don't break any laws."

I salute him and hurry out of the station.

GABE

I HURRY DOWN THE SALT-SPRINKLED SIDEWALK, THE SALT and ice crunching beneath my boots.

The snow is piled high in snowbanks between the sidewalk and the street. Romeo is only a few hours north of the city but they have a lot more snow and cold.

My breath hangs in a white fog in front of me, the chill deep, the snow falling in fat flakes. I parked down the block, not far from City Hall.

The clock tower strikes noon and a high ringing bell marks the hour, after a moment the bells begin to play "Deck the Halls."

Main Street is full of last-minute Christmas shoppers, and the smell of cinnamon and ginger hangs in the air around the bakery. The last of the Christmas trees are gone from in front of the hardware shop, and as the wind blows up another gust of snow, I pull my scarf tight and start to run.

I take the stone steps two at a time, the snowflakes swirling around, and reach for the brass handle of City Hall's front door. As I do they swing wide and there in front of me is Natalie.

She steps out into the cold, her mouth forming a surprised O. Her eyes widen and then she gives me a wide smile.

"You came back."

I step forward, my gaze snagging on the bright red of her lips, the velvet red of her dress beneath her wool coat and snowflake scarf. The snow falls around her, catching in her dark curls, making her look like a Christmas angel.

"How was jail?" I ask, stepping closer, backing her toward the snow-covered stone wall.

She takes a step back, and another, until her back hits the wall. I put my hands on either side of her leaning in, pressing my warmth over her.

"Did you come to rescue me?" She tilts her head, her green eyes warm, like we're cuddling in front of the fire, the tree lit up beside us.

"I did. Where were you going in such a hurry?"

"Back to New York. To tie you up and drag you home for Christmas. Why'd you leave?"

I lean close, press my mouth to the edge of her lips, and grip the cold stone on either side of her.

"I gave my office the next few days off." I kiss the other side of her mouth. "I halted the Hudson Apartment plans and pivoted for renovation instead." I feel her smile beneath my mouth as I press a kiss to the center of her lips. "I gave money to the charity you liked so much." A bubble of laughter slips from her and I kiss her again.

"What about the play?"

I sift my fingers through her soft curls, pulling her closer, "What play?"

"Craig's Christmas play? How'd you fix that?"

I groan. She must be talking about Nicola asking to take a half-day off for Craig's play. "Craig is Nicola's cockatoo. He performs a play at his exclusive cockatoo day care three times a week. She asks to leave early every other day."

"I'm sorry. Did you say cockatoo?"

I grin and pull her in for a kiss. "Would you not have stuffed me in your trunk if you'd known that?"

"Maybe not," she grumbles. "I thought you hated children."

"I like kids. Especially my niece and nephew. I spoil them rotten. You're going to love them. We're having Christmas dinner with them." I kiss a line up her jaw, tasting the cold snow air and a hint of gingerbread. "Did you have gingerbread pancakes for breakfast?"

"Waffles." She frowns at me.

"Are there any left over?"

"Hang on," she says, pushing me back. "You went back to New York so my neighbors wouldn't be evicted."

I nod.

"And so you could give money to charity?"

I nod again.

"And to give all your staff Christmas off?"

"Yes."

"And to accept an invitation for Christmas dinner with your niece and nephew?"

"You want to meet them, right?"

"Beyond a doubt." She wraps her arms around my shoulders and asks, "Do you want to go back to the cabin? My mom's making a honey glazed ham, mashed potatoes, and green beans with our Christmas cake for dessert. If you get the star you can make a wish."

I pick Natalie up. She laughs and wraps her legs around me as I carry her back down the stairs to my car. "And if I don't get the star?"

She buries her face in my neck, kissing me. "I'll still let you make a wish."

She doesn't need to. After a reunion with her family where I confirm that I am not an actor, I'm Natalie's soul mate, we gather around the festively set table and have Christmas Eve dinner. When we eat the cake, I find the star in my piece and I make a wish.

NATALIE

DECEMBER 25, 7:01 AM

I WAKE TO THE WARMTH OF GABE'S ARMS AROUND ME.

The morning light drifts across the room and I turn onto my back, the sheets rustling over me.

Gabe's already awake, he's watching me with a kid-on-Christmas-morning kind of smile. He reaches over and brushes my hair out of my face, running his fingers over my cheek.

Soon we'll be able to smell Christmas morning cinnamon rolls baking and coffee brewing.

Overnight, I'm sure my dad laid out presents under the tree. I'm certain even when we're all old with grandkids of our own, my dad will still be playing Santa. It's really a sight to see though. The tree lit up, presents wrapped with big gold bows, cinnamon rolls steaming on the coffee table, the fire crackling, and carols playing.

Last night Gabe hung his heart ornament on our tree.

"I wish I had another gift for you," I say, shifting closer to him.

I'm in a soft fleece Christmas pajama set, thrown on last night after a long, languorous bout of love-making. Gabe's in a pair of Christmas pajama bottoms and a t-shirt. Both are an early present from Grandma, which she handed out last night after dinner.

I smooth my hand over Gabe's hair, rearranging the mess I made last night when I tugged him down to me.

"You are my gift," Gabe says, pulling me against him.

"Merry Christmas," I say, kissing him.

His drags his tongue over my lips, tasting me, and with a groan pulls back. "Merry Christmas."

"Do you love it now?"

He sits up, taking my hand in his, the sheets pooling around us. "I love Christmas because it reminds me of you."

"In what way?" I take his hands and he threads his fingers through mine.

"It's generous, open-hearted, loving...come outside."

"What?" I shake my head.

"Come outside with me. I have a present for you."

I dress in my red sweater and jeans, and Gabe pulls on his jeans, sweater and boots brought up from New York, and then we tiptoe through the house, through the kitchen and out the back door.

When we do, Gabe leans down next to the outdoor outlet and plugs in a green cord. At that the line of balsam firs surrounding the cabin lights up with red, green, yellow and orange Christmas lights.

The rising sun sends shafts of light over the sparking trees and paints the snow a glittering gold. The air is crisp, a bright winter cold. The wind whistles over the snow and a cardinal chirps a cheerful song. It's beautiful. It's so beautiful.

"When did you do this?" I ask, turning to Gabe.

But he isn't where I expect him, instead he's bending on one knee, deep in the snow. He's holding a red velvet box in his hand.

I drop into the snow next to him, the snow crunching under my knees, the cold seeping through my jeans. "Are you proposing?"

He flips open the box to reveal a ring with rubies and emeralds, the green and red bright. "The second I laid eyes on you I wanted to spend the rest of my life with you. I want to spend this Christmas with you, and next Christmas, and all the Christmases after that. I want every day with you. I love your heart, your spirit, I love you. Will you marry me?"

"Yes," I whisper, then I jump into Gabe's arms, knocking him back into the snow. "Yes. Yes."

He laughs, looking up at me from the white snow, and slips the ring on my finger. I look into his eyes and they fill with want and need and love.

"Aww, kiss her already! In my day—"

"Grandma!" I shout.

Sure enough, at the open kitchen window my grandma, my mom, my dad and Felix crowd around, watching Gabe propose. Grandma gives us a thumbs up and my parents wave. Felix just shakes his head.

Gabe grins at me. I grin back.

"Well?" I ask.

He pulls me down on top of him, the heat of his mouth overwhelming me. At that, the kitchen window slams and the curtains draw shut.

I laugh into Gabe's mouth and he pulls me in for more.

We kiss in the snow, surrounded by Christmas lights, and Christmas trees, and Christmas joy.

EPILOGUE
GABE

CHRISTMAS DAY
One Year Later

THE DINING TABLE AT OUR HOME IS EXTENDED TO SEAT sixteen, and yellow candlelight flickers and glows over the white lace tablecloth and the mistletoe and red Christmas bulb centerpieces.

The table is full of Christmas delights—roast turkey, glazed ham, mashed potatoes with gravy, wild rice with cranberries, stuffing with toasted pecans, and a gingerbread house that Natalie and I decorated last night —all spread out on Christmas china.

Everyone is here, seated around the table, passing around the dishes of food. Natalie's parents, Grandma Agnes, Felix, Cecily and Dale, Jeb and June, and of course, our neighbors, Mrs. Givenchy, the Lawsons and their daughters Felicity and Bianca, and Mr. and Mrs. Tsang.

The table is full of noise, laughter and savory smells, overlaid with the sweet. The candlelight dances off everyone's faces, and the kids nearly glow with the excitement of the day.

I take Natalie's hand and squeeze. She rests her other hand over mine and sends me that smile that hasn't failed yet in wrapping around my heart and tugging me closer to her.

If we weren't surrounded by all our family and friends I'd pick her up, carry her to the living room, and kiss her under the mistletoe hanging near the Christmas tree.

This year, Natalie positioned mistletoe in all the best places—at the front door, by the tree, at the door to our bedroom, over our bed...

She grins at me when she sees where my thoughts are taking me.

I wink.

"Merry Christmas everyone!" Cecily says, lifting her glass of cider high.

A dozen Merry Christmases echo hers and the warmth of the oven from the kitchen and the happiness of the dining room surround me.

Never in all my life would I have imagined a Christmas so full of friends and family and love, and it's all thanks to Natalie.

"A Christmas toast," I say, holding up my crystal glass full of mulled wine, "to friends, to family, to—"

There's a sharp knock on the door. I turn toward the sound, an insistent rapping.

"I'll get it," Natalie says, pushing back from the table, her red velvet dress, the one I love, glistening in the candlelight.

I listen to her footsteps fade over the wood floors and lift my glass again, "I was going to say to my wife Natalie, the reason we're all gathered here, and the reason we're about to have the best Christmas feast ever prepared, but I'll wait until she gets back—"

Natalie hurries back into the room, her face pale, her eyes wide, she stops at the edge of the table, her eyes flashing from me to Cecily then back again. I stand, take a step toward her, when she says, "They found him."

I stop. The room goes quiet. Everyone looks to Natalie.

Cecily half stands.

"Where?" I ask, moving toward her again. I take her hands.

She smiles, a Christmas smile, a hopeful smile and says, "He's in Romeo."

I pull Natalie to me, wrap her in my arms, then spin her around the room. She laughs. Behind me I can hear Cecily crying, Dale comforting her, the kids questioning.

"Thank you," I say, dropping Natalie back to the floor, wrapping her hand in mine.

"For what?" she asks, smiling up at me, her cheeks flushed.

"For opening my heart, for letting in all this light. For marrying me. For helping me find my brother."

"Miss Erma was right, wasn't she?" Natalie asks, leaning close, the soft velvet of her dress running over me.

"About what?"

"She said all I had to do was get you to Romeo for Christmas and it would fix everything."

I nod solemnly. "Then yes. She was right."

And in all the years to come, all the Christmases in front of me, I can see that she was right about it all. Natalie and I together, Christmas magic filling our lives.

"Are you going to Romeo tonight?" Cecily asks over the talking and the excitement.

Natalie squeezes my hand and I nod. "Yes. We're going."

After all, Christmas is the day magic happens, and Romeo is where magic begins.

As Natalie and I leave, I pause under the door, the mistletoe above us, and I gather her in my arms. "Merry Christmas," I say, brushing a kiss over her lips.

"Merry Christmas," she says.

And it is. They all are. The happiest, merriest most wonderful Christmases that I've ever known. We've found Lee. We finally found him.

Then we hurry into the starry night, snowflakes falling, the bells on our front door ringing, the snow sparkling under the streetlamps, a wish in my heart, a Christmas wish that has finally come true.

"Want to climb in the trunk for old time's sake?" Natalie asks.

I lift an eyebrow, pulling her down the sidewalk. "Try it and I'll tie you to the bed with Christmas lights."

Her laugh sounds like bells. Then we hurry to the car and drive out of the city to Romeo and to Christmas wishes that come true.

THE END

GET A BONUS EPILOGUE

Want more Natalie and Gabe? Get an exclusive bonus epilogue for newsletter subscribers only.

When you join the Sarah Ready Newsletter you get access to sneak peaks, insider updates, exclusive bonus scenes and more.

Join Today!

www.sarahready.com/newsletter

ABOUT THE AUTHOR

Author Sarah Ready writes contemporary romance and romantic comedy. Her books have been described as "euphoric", "heartwarming" and "laugh out loud". Her debut novel *The Fall in Love Checklist* was hailed as "the unicorn read of 2020".

Sarah writes stand-alone romcoms and romcoms in the Soulmates in Romeo series, all of which can be found at her website: www.sarahready.com.

Stay up to date, get exclusive epilogues and bonus content. Join Sarah's newsletter at www.sarahready.com/newsletter.

ALSO BY SARAH READY

Stand Alone Romances:

The Fall in Love Checklist

Hero Ever After

Once Upon an Island

Josh and Gemma Make a Baby

Josh and Gemma the Second Time Around

Soul Mates in Romeo Romance Series:

Chasing Romeo

Love Not at First Sight

Romance by the Book

Love, Artifacts, and You

Married by Sunday

My Better Life

Scrooging Christmas

Stand Alone Novella:

Love Letters

Find these books and more by Sarah Ready at:

www.sarahready.com/romance-books